Amy t____ _____ ____nt of
her, and eased into the living room. On the floor by the
glass patio doors, a six-foot feather palm sprawled atop
strewn black soil. A lacy Ming Aralia and a green-
veined white caladium hung limply from empty porcelain pots.

She shivered. The killer hadn't yet found what he
wanted. Amy moved from room to room, opening
drapes, throwing open closet doors, and checking behind furniture.

At last satisfied she was alone in the house, she
changed into jeans, donned gloves and knee pads, and
began an inspection of the polished wood floors. Mai's
barefooted killer had to have left a sole print.

An hour's search turned up several clear ones in the
living room. She set a camcorder on a tripod to pan the
area, positioned an overturned coffee can containing a
sixty-watt bulb near the print, inverted a small fish tank
over that, and set a fingerprint camera down on the floor
within arm's reach.

At some point in her routine, Amy got the distinct
feeling that she was being watched. Without lifting her
head, she checked the patio doors. Nothing. Rising, she
pretended to reach for her forensic satchel but instead
grabbed the camcorder handle and swung it toward the
front windows.

Fear ballooned in her chest.

A snarling man in a black hood was crouched in the
shrubbery.

Louise Hendricksen (signature)

Louise Hendricksen

LETHAL LEGACY

ZEBRA BOOKS
KENSINGTON PUBLISHING CORP.

ZEBRA BOOKS are published by

Kensington Publishing Corp.
850 Third Avenue
New York, NY 10022

Zebra and the Z logo Reg. U.S. Pat. & TM Off.

First Printing: June, 1995

Printed in the United States of America

To my good friend Stella Cameron—a wise woman who knows when to push and when to praise.

1

Murder spawned a stench all its own.

Dr. Amy Prescott flipped a switch, casting the murky kitchen into stark relief. *Blood was everywhere.* Obscene sprays, spatters and splotches of it.

Mai Nguyen's blood.

Mai, wife of Dr. Cam Nguyen, Amy's colleague, her trusted friend.

Amy sagged against the doorjamb. "Poor little Mai."

Wind moaned a dirge through the house. Somewhere in the distance, Amy fancied she heard a woman sobbing.

Dr. B.J. Prescott put his arm around his daughter. "You sure you want to be in on this?"

Amy sighed wearily, then glared at Sheriff Fred Boyce, who had wedged his stocky body in the doorway. "Cam didn't kill her and I intend to prove it."

Boyce narrowed his eyes and thrust out his beefy chin. "Nguyen's in jail and he's gonna stay there. The man was covered with her blood. What more do ya want?"

B.J. ran the heel of his hand over the strip of gray hair fringing his bald pate and said in a controlled voice,

"He's an M.D. There's no way you can treat a bleeding patient without getting some on you."

"Might a known you doctors would stick together." Boyce leaned on a counter, putting his hands behind him to grip the edge.

Amy, stooping to slip white paper booties over her shoes, caught his movement. "Don't touch that," she said sharply.

Boyce straightened and dropped his arms, his face turning red. "Where the hell do you get off telling me what to do?"

Amy, her voluminous white coveralls a contrast to the blood-spattered room, faced him squarely. "We're here to investigate a murder. Or have you forgotten that?"

B.J. put his hand on his daughter's arm in a calming gesture, then stepped out onto the back porch and retrieved his and Amy's forensic kits. "We'll need a copy of your prints and those of your deputy and the paramedics." Then he sat down on the edge of a chair, bending over his midriff to tug on his shoe covers.

Sheriff Boyce grunted and shifted his feet. "No need of those paramedics even being here. The woman was dead."

Amy lifted her gaze from the viewfinder of her camera. "Cam's attorney told me she was conscious when Cam found her."

"That's what *Nguyen* says. I figure he started battin' her around and she fought back. He grabbed a knife out of that rack over there"—he gestured toward a slotted wooden block—"killed her, dragged her into the bedroom, then called the paramedics to make it look as if he'd just come home and found her that way."

B.J. took a box of tacks and a ball of string from the

pocket of his white coveralls. "Did you find the weapon?"

Boyce hooked his thumbs over the belt of his khaki-colored pants and rocked on his heels. "The way I see it, he washed the knife and stuck it back where it come from. I took all of 'em in as evidence."

Amy raked her fingers through her short-cut brown hair and sighed exasperatedly. "So now your prints are all over the knife rack."

"Watch it, girl." The sheriff pointed a stubby finger at her. "I've about had it with you."

B.J. caught his daughter's eye. "Let's divide the kitchen into quadrants. We've got a whopper of a job ahead of us." He swung around to Boyce. "I assume you took pictures of the body before you let them move her."

"Pictures! When the hell was I gonna take pictures? Christ, Nguyen had a hold a her and wouldn't let go. Had to pry him loose." The man folded his arms obstinately. "Ain't got a camera, anyway. Wheeler isn't full of rich folks like you got in Ursa Bay."

B.J. didn't bother to respond. He fastened a loop of string around a tack, pushed it into the baseboard, and tossed the ball of string to Amy.

"Well," said the sheriff. "I guess I'll let you two get on with whatever it is you do." He let out a short, derisive laugh, turned, and left the house.

Any blew her hair out of her eyes, rolled her eyes in exasperation, then edged around the room. Kneeling, she stretched the line her father had thrown her taut, and fastened it at the base of a cabinet.

Having gone through the procedure many times before, B.J. and Amy worked with practiced precision. As soon as they finished, B.J. plugged in a small evidence vacuum and started cleaning the floor.

Meanwhile, Amy took pictures of bloodstain patterns on the cabinets and floor, following the tracks where Mai's slender fingers had slid down the white wall, the dark trails on the gleaming blue vinyl floor-covering.

Visions of the murderer dragging Mai feet first, her long, black, blood-wet hair streaming out behind her, rose in Amy's mind. The room tilted, started to spin. She staggered to a chair and put her head down between her knees.

B.J. switched off the vacuum. "You okay?"

Amy shook her head. "Lord, I'm nearly four months along. I thought I'd be over it by now."

B.J.'s eyes turned a frosty blue and his lips thinned. "You wanted to be a mother."

Amy jerked upright and glared at him. Did he have to start in on her now, of all times? Always, the same old theme. She'd been hearing it ever since she'd told him she was pregnant with Nathan Blackthorn's child. "Skip it, Dad. I'm not in the mood."

B.J. shook his head, then turned on the vacuum and went back to his task of collecting, packaging, and labeling a filter disk for each quadrant.

Amy gritted her teeth. Lectures and looks, she'd had her fill of them. Good God, a woman over thirty ought to know what was right for her. She snatched up the ball of twine. "I'm going to start on the living room," she said, gesturing to him over the hum of the vacuum.

Amy moved through the doorway and assessed the scene, letting her mind absorb each detail. One drape dangled from a twisted rod, letting in a slice of bleary light and the *rata-tat-tat* of wind-driven rain on the glass. On bare flooring, a porcelain table lamp lay in a fragmented starburst of opalescent blue. Nearby, a white satin chair had been pushed over on its side. By the front door, an askew Oriental carpet—blue and white in squared lineal patterns. Each article a reminder of Mai and her impeccable taste.

Amy shook herself and began to section off the space. She had to keep her wits about her today. Had to stay in control of her emotions.

Slowly, painstakingly, Amy and her father worked their way through the rambling one-story house. According to forensic theorists, a murderer always brings something to a crime scene—even though it may be microscopic in size—and takes something away. At this scene, they were at a disadvantage. No documentation had been done at the time of discovery and too many people had been allowed to come and go since the murder.

It was after one o'clock when B.J. peered into the master bedroom. "What do you make of all those archaeology books in the study? They sure look technical."

Amy shut off the vacuum. "I have no idea. Cam never mentioned any interest in archaeology during our residency together." She rose, stepped over the twine she'd strung, and set the vacuum down in the hall. "Maybe they belonged to Mai's father. This used to be his house." She frowned and chewed the edge of her lip.

"Does Mai's father still live in Wheeler?"

Amy looked up in surprise. "Didn't I tell you? He was killed in a hit-and-run last June. They never did find the driver."

"Hmmm, I don't remember hearing about it," B.J. said. "What was his name?"

"Chantou Pran. Intelligent man. I met him at Mai and Cam's wedding."

"Mai have any other family?"

Amy shook her head. "Her mother died in Cambodia shortly after Mai was born."

B.J. inspected a white oak highboy. Cam's shorts, T-shirts, socks, and sweaters dangled from half-open drawers and littered the floor below. He moved on to a mirrored dresser. A cultured pearl necklace and a tangle of gold chains spilled over the edge of a teak wood box. "He went through everything, but didn't take the expensive stuff. Why would he do that?"

"There's also no sign of forced entry."

B.J. stroked his graying mustache and Vandyke beard. "Do you think she let him in?"

"Might have. Country folks aren't as suspicious of strangers as city folks."

"He might not have been a stranger."

"Possible." Amy removed her glasses, rubbed her weary eyes, and pointed to a dent in one of the bed pillows. "Looks like Mai was in bed. She must have gotten up to answer the doorbell."

"Right. There's a peephole in both doors. So, it's likely she did know the guy."

Anguish twisted Amy's features. "Unless she got up when Cam let himself in."

B.J.'s eyes softened with compassion. "Have to consider the possibility, kitten."

"I know, I know," she said softly.

B.J. blew several puffs of breath along the dresser's gleaming top. "Got some weak prints here. Let's fume it." He readjusted his respirator.

Amy donned a self-contained breathing apparatus. Since learning she was pregnant, she'd taken more care than usual not to inhale the various elements they handled on the job.

B.J. wrapped his hand around the glass fumer to heat the silver iodine crystals, while Amy readied the Folmer-Graflex print camera. "All set?" he asked. When she nodded, B.J. squeezed the fumer's air bulb. Purple smoke floated out of the glass tube and spread across the dresser top. Brown latents popped up all over the polished surface.

After taking the views she needed, Amy laid a flexible sheet of silver over the latents—iodine reacted with the silver, creating near perfect prints. Buoyed by their success, she turned to another area of the room. When she tired, she sat back on her heels and watched her father.

With practiced ease, B.J. dusted nightstands and louvered closet doors with bichromatic powder. Using hinged, transparent lifters, he transferred prints to three-by-five-inch index cards. When he glanced up and saw her observing him, he smiled. "About done?"

"Getting there." Amy groaned, caught hold of a chair, and pulled herself up. Her back ached, her feet hurt, and she had a catch in her left side, but she wasn't finished yet.

She sighed and hooked the strap of her 35-millimeter camera around her neck. Better get on with it. She labeled a paper evidence bag and put on a pair of latex gloves. In a corner, she picked up Mai's wadded nightgown and dropped it into the prepared sack.

As the green satin gown slithered through her fingers, images of a man repeatedly stabbing Mai flashed through her mind. She shuddered as goose bumps rose on her arms.

Despite the room's spring-like decor of pale peach

and willow green, an evil aura pervaded the atmosphere. She could smell the fear, feel the terror, the terrible pain.

With an effort, Amy pulled her thoughts together and snapped pictures of marks where Mai's blood-soaked nightgown had struck the wall and slid down. Then she turned to the brown encrusted pools of blood on the parquet floor.

When at last she straightened, she glanced out the window and noticed Sheriff Boyce sitting outside in his patrol car, eating his lunch. "*Sheriff!* That's a laugh. Some example of law enforcement," she muttered. She slammed her forensic kit closed. "No pictures. Not even a sketch of the room or an outline of where she lay." She swung around to her father. "Dammit, Dad, we don't even know if Mai was raped."

B.J. put his arm around his daughter's shoulders. "Easy, honey. The coroner agreed to have her body transferred to our lab. We'll have a lot more answers when we do the postmortem tomorrow."

2

Amy sat on a high stool surrounded by glass-doored cabinets lined with instruments, electric saws, and large glass jars containing various preserved organs. Ceiling and wall vent fans hummed. The red ON lights of an overhead camera and microphone blinked. Below, on a steel autopsy table equipped with running water, lay the body of Mai Nguyen.

Strips of toweling covered her breasts and pubic area—her modesty respected for the moment. Except for plum-colored bruises, purple-edged gashes, and patches of dried blood, Mai resembled a diminutive porcelain statue, with perfect proportions and exquisite features. So young, so gentle, what could possibly have provoked someone to kill her? Amy thought.

She dabbed her forehead and face with a damp paper towel. The nausea she'd experienced that morning was again assaulting her in waves.

B.J. finished laying out his instruments and eyed her speculatively. "Feeling okay?"

"Not really."

He rested a hand on her shoulder. "Isn't it about time you saw someone?"

"I have an appointment in Seattle tomorrow." She wet her dry lips. "Do you mind if I don't assist?"

"The coroner can help. Time he learned to do a proper post anyhow."

Amy ran over the familiar procedure in her mind. An inch-by-inch inspection of the body with a high-power magnifying lens; a careful combing of pubic hair; examination of the vaginal vault; slides and samples from under fingernails and from every orifice. A total body fuming with cyanoacrylate inside a vinyl tent to bring out fingerprints. Another inspection—this time in the dark with the aid of an ultraviolet light; a head-to-toe dusting with black fingerprint powder, and a final going-over with a high-intensity light.

After all this, her father would pick up a scalpel to make the "Y" section. A clean slash from each clavicle to the base of the sternum, then another from sternum to pubis.

She gazed over at Mai's body. "Use barium sulfate in the knife wounds and take plenty of X-rays. If it doesn't give a good outline, pour some melted Wood's metal into them. That may give us the size and shape of the blade."

B.J. grinned and laugh lines fanned out over his ruddy cheeks. "Yes, Dr. Prescott, I believe I know the routine. Now go on about your business. Kibitzers make me nervous."

Amy made a face at him and went upstairs to her apartment. While drinking a cup of herbal tea, her mind wandered as it frequently did to Nathan Blackthorn. Nathan had given her some terrible-tasting concoction the night she was poisoned. If he were here, maybe he'd have an Indian remedy for nausea. But he wasn't here; would never, ever be here. The thought made her ache.

Foolishness. She seized the phone, called Cam's attorney, and asked him to arrange for her to meet with Cam. That done, she took the elevator down to the office and buried herself in paperwork for a couple of hours. By ten o'clock, she felt strong enough to make the thirty-five-mile trip to Wheeler.

The jail was on the first floor of the red-brick courthouse. After passing by offices marked CITY CLERK, HOUSING AUTHORITY, and PUBLIC WORKS, she approached a glass door. Large black letters trimmed in gold assured her she had arrived at the sheriff's department.

She opened the door quietly and peeked inside. Two once-white fixtures in a twelve-foot, water-stained ceiling provided feeble illumination. In front of a gray metal locker flanked by two file cabinets sat a man in his middle twenties. He had his chair tipped back and his ragged athletic shoes propped on a pulled-out drawer.

When Amy closed the office door, the man hastily lowered his feet and bent over a stack of papers on the desk. She approached a counter that bisected the room. After she'd stood there for several minutes, the young man raised his head, pushed thick-lensed glasses farther up on his long nose, and brought her into focus.

"You want something?"

"I'm Dr. Amy Prescott, one of the investigators on the Nguyen case. I came to talk with Dr. Nguyen."

The man pushed aside a flap of lank, blond hair. "No visitors allowed." He got up, turned his back to her, and started pawing through a file drawer.

Amy stared at him with disbelief. "Young Man? . . ."

He wheeled around and marched over to the counter.

"The name's Pierce, lady." He puffed out his skinny chest. "Deputy Duane Pierce."

Amy managed a smile and stuck out her hand. "Good morning, Deputy Pierce. Jed MacManus, Dr. Nguyen's attorney, called Sheriff Boyce this morning and got permission for me to see Dr. Nguyen."

"Nobody told me," the man said skeptically.

"Is Sheriff Boyce in?"

Deputy Pierce gestured widely about the room. "Do you see him?"

Amy reined in her temper. "Would you locate him for me please?"

"He's in a meeting."

Amy clenched her teeth. Some meeting. She'd seen the sheriff's patrol car parked in front of Myra's Restaurant on her way through town. "Doesn't Sheriff Boyce have a two-way radio?"

"He doesn't like being disturbed when he's, uh . . . when he's in a meeting."

Amy sat down determinedly in a chair. "I'm afraid we're going to just have to upset him a little then, aren't we?" she said.

Half an hour later, Sheriff Boyce lumbered into the office and yelled, "Doo*wayne,* how many times I told you not to bother me when I'm over at My"—he caught sight of Amy and halted, then glowered—"I mighta known." Boyce stomped behind the counter. "Deputy Pierce, put Nguyen in the visiting room." He jerked his head at Amy. "Stick *her* in the hall."

Amy sat on a wooden bench and waited. She watched as, from somewhere in the murky reaches of the dimly lit hall, an Asian man appeared, shoving a damp mop back and forth over bilious green vinyl. He moved slowly along the corridor toward her.

When he was about twenty feet from her, he lifted his head. Amy noticed a puckered scar that extended from his right cheekbone to his ear. His eyes met hers—jet black and cold as a cobra's. A chill ran through her. She clutched her purse and silently willed the deputy to hurry.

After what seemed an eternity, Deputy Pierce sauntered out of the gloom and came up behind the man with the mop. "Get your ass in gear, Sen. You gotta swab out Nguyen's cage."

Pierce snickered, opened a door, and motioned Amy inside. "Don't be passing any stuff to him, ya hear?" He said sarcastically, then propped himself in the open doorway and took a folded comic book from his back pocket.

The gray, windowless room had an entrance at either end. A table-height partition topped with a four-foot wide counter extended from wall to wall. Cam slumped in a chair on one side of the barrier.

Amy took her seat and peered at the man. Even when they'd worked double shifts as interns, he'd always managed to appear neat and well groomed. Now, he had mussed hair, rumpled clothing, and the skin covering his fine-boned features had taken on a greenish cast.

"Cam." She put her hand out as far as she could but still couldn't reach him. "I'm so sorry."

He let out a sigh that shook his entire body. "God, Amy. I still can't believe this is real." He looked at her with a stricken expression. "The whole thing is a nightmare."

"I know," she said gently. "Cam, I want to try to help you, to find out what happened. Are you up to answering some questions?"

"Anything . . . anything that'll make some sense out

of this. Thank God you're on the case. I really need a friend right now." He smiled weakly.

Amy opened her notebook and placed it on the counter. "Cam, some of these questions might upset you—I'm sorry. Just be assured that I believe you're innocent and I'm going to do everything in my power to help you prove that."

Cam nodded and took a deep breath. "Please, go on," he said.

"Had you and Mai been having any problems?"

Cam looked away from her sadly. "Some."

"Tell me," Amy said softly.

He ran his fingers through his hair. "I've been going over and over this for hours. I think things started falling apart about six months ago."

"What happened?"

"After Mai's father died ... I don't know, she changed."

"In what way?"

"She became withdrawn. I thought the move back to her old home, taking care of Chantou's landscape business, would help her." He swallowed and shook his head. "She got worse. Started imagining things. People following her, spying on her. She had all the locks changed twice."

Amy jotted down a few words. "Cam, did you work late Friday night?"

"No ..." Cam put his head in his hands. "If only I'd gone home, maybe ..." He met Amy's steady gaze. "I had dinner with a woman I met at the hospital. Afterwards, we went to her apartment. Nothing happened, I swear it. All we did was talk. Amy, I loved Mai."

Amy nodded her head reassuringly. "What time did you get home?"

Cam glanced at her, then away. "About twelve-thirty."

Amy recorded the time. "Where was Mai?"

His mouth trembled as he tried to get himself under control. "She was . . . lying naked on the floor of our bedroom." His dark eyes grew moist. "Amy, Mai wouldn't let anyone see her naked . . ." He gulped. "We were married two years before she even let me."

Amy nodded. "I remember you telling me she refused even to wear tennis shorts."

"Most old-country Cambodian girls are like that."

"What did you do after you found Mai?"

"So much blood. God, it was all over her. I tried to stop the bleeding"—his voice broke—"Then her . . . her heart stopped and . . . I tried to resuscitate her." He raised his eyes to meet hers. "I save other people's lives all day long." He beat his fist on the counter. "But I couldn't save my own wife."

"Don't do this to yourself, Cam. I've seen you work. I know you did everything you could to save her."

"It didn't keep her from dying."

"If you couldn't help her, nobody could." She gave him a moment to compose himself, then spoke again. "Let's go back to this woman you were with. Will she testify you were together?"

Cam pressed his fingers into his temples and shook his head. "It's the strangest thing. The sheriff says he went to the apartment to check my story. The manager told him he'd never heard of Chea Le, that apartment 105 is only used for display and it's never been rented by anyone."

Amy blew out her breath. "That *is* strange . . ."

Cam sat forward. "Amy, do you still believe me?"

"Of course, I—" As Amy started to reassure him, she

heard the clank of a bucket in the hallway and remembered the man with the chilling stare. "Just a second," she said impulsively. She got up, leaned around Deputy Pierce, and glanced out. Mop in one hand, bucket in the other, the janitor was shuffling down the hall.

She turned to the deputy. "Has that man been outside this door ever since we started talking?"

"Huh?" The deputy lowered his comic book. "What man?"

She rounded on him, her brown eyes blazing. "The one you called Sen."

The deputy smirked. "No reason to get all het-up. He's only the janitor."

"It's your job to keep this meeting confidential. Whoever he is, he can broadcast Cam's story all over the Southeast Asian community you . . . you . . ." When the man smiled at her coolly, Amy made a sound of disgust, then seated herself opposite Cam again and tried to retrieve her train of thought.

"Is this Chea Le a nurse at the hospital?"

"No. She's a volunteer," Cam said.

"What do you know about her?"

"We only went out that one time. She told me that she and her boyfriend had quarreled. We shared our troubles."

"The administration office should have some information on her, shouldn't they?"

He shrugged. "Volunteers are a hospital fixture. I can't remember even speaking to one before I met Chea."

While Amy scribbled a reminder to call Harborview Medical Center in Seattle, her mind hit upon a far-fetched notion. "You're Vietnamese, aren't you, Cam?"

"Ethnically speaking, but my father's family lived in

Cambodia for generations. And as you know, my mother is Caucasian."

"How do Cambodians feel about the Vietnamese?"

"There's hostility on both sides." He grimaced. "Khmers call the Vietnamese barbarians. The Vietnamese call the Khmers lazy."

"Khmers?"

Cam's heavy brows knotted in an irritated frown. " 'Cambodia' is a name the French and English tacked on the country. Natives think of themselves as Khmers and their country as Kampuchea. Where is all this going, Amy?"

"I'm searching for a motive."

He stared at her, his eyes wide. "A blood feud? Good God, Amy, that's ridiculous."

"Do you have a better idea? Who had a reason to kill Mai?"

Cam winced and turned his head.

"Cam?" Amy said. *"Is there someone you suspect?"*

"She was . . ." Cam's head drooped and he bit his lip.

"Was what? Don't hold out on me, Cam. I need to know everything, no matter how hard this is for you."

He expelled a long sigh. "I saw her not too long ago with a man."

"Who was he? Did you know him?"

"No. I mean, I don't know. I never saw his face."

"Where did you see them? What were they doing?"

"On the street. I followed her one day. She'd been acting so strange. It looked as if they were arguing." He jumped to his feet. "Dammit, Amy, what's the point of going into all this? Nobody's going to believe me."

"Let my father and me be the ones to worry about that. Did you ask Mai about the man you saw her with?"

"She wouldn't tell me anything. Not his name or what they'd been talking about or what he meant to her. Nothing. All she did was cry."

Amy started to close her notebook, then changed her mind. "Cam, did Mai say anything to you before she died?"

"Only two words." Cam slumped down on the chair. "Sounded like, 'My garden.' "

"That mean anything to you?"

His face softened. "Mai loved her topiary garden. Her father started it when she was a child. And even when he had to labor fourteen hours a day to keep his business going, he still found time to work on the animals he created for her."

He traced a scratch in the countertop with his fingernail. "Funny thing though, after she moved back home, she wouldn't go near the garden. One day, she even went into hysterics when I tried to coax her inside."

Amy finished her notes and stood up. "I'm going to wander through town and ask some questions. Got any ideas who I should talk to?"

He shook his head. "When we were going together, Mai used to visit with practically everyone we met. Since her father died, she's scarcely seen anyone. Lately, she even refused to go into town for groceries."

Amy slipped her notebook into her purse. "I'll do some checking and get back to you in a few days. Is bail being arranged?"

"What money we have is tied up. I'm stuck here."

"Hang in there, Cam. I'll do everything I can to help you." She gave Cam a thumbs-up sign and left.

The next two hours proved to be an exercise in frustration. Questions she addressed to shop owners and people on the street produced nothing but shrugs and impassive looks. Finally she gave up and started home.

She had crossed the Wasku River before she took any notice of the blue pickup truck behind her. After about ten miles had passed, she saw that the vehicle was still the same distance behind her. Smiling at herself for being paranoid, she slowed down. The truck kept the same amount of space between them. When she sped up, so did the other driver. She decided to get serious. Doing sixty around curves that weren't safe at thirty-five, she tried to shake him. No way would she let him follow her home.

She and her father had discovered that being forensic investigators had a down side. People they helped convict sometimes sought revenge. Now, they met clients at places other than the office. They maintained a post office box for their mail and kept their address out of the phone book.

She zoomed down a straight stretch of highway. The station wagon's tires drilling asphalt, she whipped onto a graveled side road and barreled down a winding lane hemmed by tall fir trees. She made a hard left at the intersection. When she'd reached the farmhouse, she turned up the rutted driveway and stopped among screening evergreens. Her pulse thundering in her ears, she waited.

Minutes later, a blue pickup flashed by.

3

Twins! Amy folded her sheet of instructions and left the specialist's office in a rosy daze. Now she'd have two of Nathan's children instead of only one—a double blessing, since they would be the only reminder she'd have of him.

Three months ago, Nathan had married a woman of his own race. He'd given Amy plenty of warning. Told her of his impending wedding. Spoken of his white mother's untimely death and the judgment his grief-stricken father had made: white women were weak, Indian women are strong. His father had drummed his convictions into Nathan, along with the admonishment not to dilute his Native American bloodline any further.

She pictured Nathan's firm, resolute face and couldn't help loving him, despite the pain he'd caused her. She sighed, rested her head against the wall of the elevator, and wondered if Nathan was still so sure he'd done the right thing.

When she exited the building and glimpsed the weak but welcome January sun, her mood lightened. The news about the twins called for a celebration.

She strolled up Seattle's Fifth Avenue and entered the

plushly carpeted lobby of the Maxfield Hotel. On her way to the dining room, she passed a reader board. In letters so small she had to squint to read them, the management discretely welcomed members of "The Resort Owner's Association." She smiled and hoped the convention participants had better eyesight than she did, or they'd never know where to meet.

She checked her coat. Whiffs of opulent perfumes and a murmur of genteel voices greeted her as the maître d' showed her to a table. His silver hair, black suit, and snowy white shirt complemented the elegant mauve and seafoam green decor.

Pleased that her new outfit's full, navy-blue jacket and billowy pink blouse cleverly concealed her gravid state, she settled herself on a mauve velvet chair. Picking up the gilt menu, she beamed at the other diners and silently announced, *I'm going to be the mother of twins.*

"Amy!"

At hearing her name, Amy dropped the menu from her hands. How well she knew that voice. But Nathan? She must be hallucinating; Nathan couldn't possibly be here. She glanced right and left, saw no one she recognized, and sank back in her chair. She'd have to watch herself. Although she often carried on long internal conversations with Nathan, this was the first time she'd imagined him speaking to her.

But then the voice came again. "Amy . . . ? Amy, is that . . . ?"

The sound of the familiar deep voice drawing out the syllables of her name speeded her pulse. Finally, she caught sight of him, and when she did, everyone and everything else faded into the background. Garbed in a dark gray pinstripe suit, he could have passed for a successful banker—if it weren't for his black, shoulder-length hair.

She watched him approach, noting the reaction of the men as their female companions took in the sight of Nathan—his tall, lithe form, his high cheekbones, the slight curve of his nose, his beautiful mouth.

Oblivious to their stares, he moved through the crowd, wearing a look of bemused wonderment.

When he reached her table, he stared down at her and shook his head. "This is unbelievable. You're really here."

His soft tone as he spaced each word in his usual deliberate fashion sent a shiver through her. Never in her wildest imaginings had she envisioned a meeting such as this.

She stared back at him, at a loss for what to say. "What are you doing in Seattle?" she finally uttered.

"Attending a resort owner's conference."

Understanding dawned on her face. "Yes, I saw the sign outside." She eased the white tablecloth closer to her abdomen, hoping her dress concealed her pregnancy. "Is the lodge finished then?"

"Yes," Nathan answered. He rested his hand on the chair opposite her and smiled. "Are you eating alone?"

She nodded and drew in a breath that didn't seem to fill her lungs. "Would you like to join me?"

Without taking his gaze from her face, he pulled out the chair. As he lowered himself into it, a waitress appeared. "My name is Nathan Blackthorn," he informed the woman. He took a room key from his jacket pocket. "Will you put our lunch on my room tab, please?"

"Would you like a menu, Mr. Blackthorn?"

Nathan shook his head. "I'll have whatever my companion is having."

Amy snatched up the menu. Smoked salmon croquettes, the least expensive entrée on the page, cost fifteen dollars. She gave her order and waited until the waitress moved out of earshot before whispering, "Nathan, I can't let you treat me. The prices here are sky high."

He narrowed his eyes, gave a careful look around, and leaned toward her conspiratorially. "Shh, I'm masquerading as a big-time resort owner." He broke into a grin and then laughed. "Believe me, I can afford it."

Amy remembered the faded jeans and chambray shirts he'd worn when she'd first met him in Idaho. "So it's all happening for you then."

"Yep." He chuckled, then seemed surprised the sound had come from him. "We have a good snow pack and the ski lifts are running full bore. Believe it or not, The Wahiliye is booked up until spring thaw." He smiled at her puzzled expression. "Wahiliye means Eagle Place. Do you like it?"

Smiling, she nodded and tried to pronounce the name. "It doesn't sound half as nice when I say it."

A mischievous look came into his eyes. "Want some lessons?"

She raised an eyebrow, but ignored the question. "You've only had the lodge four months. How did you manage to get it up and running so fast?"

He broke into a laugh and his eyes sparkled. "Luck, fourteen-hour days, and lots of help. I called a friend in Bavaria who used to own a resort. He flew in, liked the area, and decided to stay." He shook his head. "Mammoth job, Amy."

"Well, I guess. I'm amazed you're already operational."

"I wouldn't be if not for Franz," he said as the waitress returned with their lunch. Nathan spread his napkin over his lap and picked up his fork. "It's really wonderful though. Native Americans make up the majority of our work force. I opened a skill center to train them."

Amy tasted a spicy salmon croquette and hoped the rich meal wouldn't upset her stomach. "How did old Rock Springs react to that?"

He swallowed a forkful of salmon and smiled. "Actually, the community's been extremely welcoming. Course, there's a lot of revenue involved."

"Amazing how quickly some people forget their prejudices in the face of money. I'm glad it's working out," she said as she selected a scallop-edged slice of cucumber from the artistic nest of vegetables surrounding the two croquettes.

"How's your life going?" Nathan asked after a moment.

The question jarred her out of her reverie. *Great, just great. You're married to another woman and I'm carrying your twins.* She pursed her lips and wobbled her hand. "So so."

He lay down his fork. "Apparently you're happy."

She stiffened. Had she given herself away? She picked up a tiny carrot stick, bit off a piece, chewed, and tried to swallow. "Oh?"

Nathan pushed his plate aside and concentrated on restoring his napkin to its former pleated state. "I was on my way to the coffee shop"—he gestured toward the mezzanine—"when I heard the man in front of me say, 'that's what I call a pretty woman.' I glanced over the rail and there you were." He slowly raised his gaze to meet hers. "He didn't even come close, Amy."

The softness in his eyes undid her. "Didn't come"— she hesitated—"close?"

He smiled. "You look absolutely beautiful."

Much to her distress, her eyes filmed over. She ducked her head, blinked rapidly, and stretched her eyes wide to contain the moisture. When she thought it safe, she smiled across at him. "Thanks. A woman my age needs an occasional boost."

"Say," Nathan asked, "are you in love?"

She stayed silent for a long moment, selecting and discarding answers. "Being in love's not the only cause of happiness, Nathan."

Nathan smiled at her gently. "No." he said as his gaze moved over her face. "Not the only one." His scrutiny sharpened. "You've gained weight. That's good." He plucked a stray shred of lettuce from the tablecloth and deposited it on his abandoned plate, before he again met her eyes. "I've been worried about you."

Her throat tightened. She hoped she could keep her voice steady. "No need. I'm a tough old bird."

He lifted an eyebrow and smiled. "Sure you are. Poison couldn't kill you and bullets bounce right off your skin." Abruptly, his attention turned to a corner of the room, where a clock chimed softly. With disappointment in his eyes, he pushed back his chair and got to his feet. "I have to go. My meeting starts in a few minutes."

She laced her fingers together to keep her hands from trembling. When she spoke again, her voice sounded tight and unnatural to her ears. "Nice seeing you again. Thanks very much for lunch."

Nathan ran his thumb along the welting of the velvet chair. "Could we . . . have dinner?"

Amy stared down at her clenched hands. Much as she wanted to be with him, she knew dinner together would only compound the pain she felt over losing him. "I have to get back to Ursa Bay. I'm working on a case."

"I see . . ." He shifted his feet. "Well . . ." He sighed deeply. "It was nice talking to you, Amy."

"Yes, very nice." She spoke slowly in an effort to keep her emotions under control. "T-take care."

He smiled sadly. "You too." He started across the room, hesitated, and retraced his steps. "If you should ever need me, for anything, call me." He handed her his business card and strode out of the room.

Amy watched him leave, then sat for a few moments, gathering her thoughts. Then she picked up her purse and prepared to leave.

As she started to rise, the skin prickled at the back of her neck. She settled back in her chair. Someone was watching her, she could feel it. She surveyed the room, then finally looked up.

Nathan stood at the third floor railing, gazing down at her, a strange, unreadable expression playing across his face.

4

At 8:00 P.M. the bedside phone rang. Amy sighed, rolled over, and lifted the receiver. "This is Dr. Prescott."

"Hi, Nathan here. Am I interrupting anything?"

Her heartbeat quickened at the sound of his voice. She'd been thinking about him ever since lunch that afternoon. "No, I just crawled into bed."

"Bed!" His voice rose. "Are you sick?"

"Just tired."

"I knew it."

She forced down a surge of panic. "Knew what?"

"You haven't been well, have you?"

His statement didn't surprise her. In his early boyhood, Nathan had been taught by his grandfather to use all of his five senses. Now, they were finely honed. He could read people well.

"You needn't worry about me, Nathan."

He let out a long breath. "I saved your life once. We are spirit bonded." He sighed again. "What kind of a case are you working on? It must be a difficult one."

"It is. Dr. Cam Nguyen, a friend I interned with, has been accused of murdering his wife."

"Did he do it?"

"No, but so far everything seems to suggest the opposite. And his alibi has completely fallen through."

"Whoa, hold it a second," Nathan said. Amy heard a couple of thumps and a rustle of fabric through the phone line, followed by a soft chuckle. "All settled in. Start at the beginning. I want to hear everything."

During her detailed account of the murder and investigation up to that point, Nathan stopped her occasionally to ask a question. When she came to the end of her discussion, he inhaled deeply, then laughed. "I never thought I would get the itch again," he said. "But I would sure like to be working on this with you."

"Well, it's a tough one, all right. As soon as I find someone in Wheeler's Southeast Asian community who'll talk to me, we'll make faster progress, I'm sure."

"Hey, I have an idea. Will you be in your office around ten tomorrow morning?"

"Yes," Amy said after a brief hesitation.

"Good. I'll meet you there, okay? See you then."

"Wait—" Any said, then realized he'd already hung up. *Damn!* She dropped the receiver back in the cradle and flopped back on the pillow. How could he possibly meet her at the office? He didn't even have the address.

Suddenly, excitement swept aside her momentary gloom. Nathan knew everything about her—her age, her birthday, even the fact that she had once been married for four years. And what he didn't know he had ways and means to find out. Last October, before they'd even met, someone in the government had provided him with a complete file on her.

* * *

The next morning, Amy tossed outfit after outfit onto her bed. She tried on every item before she chose green slacks and a matching jacket that went well with her brown hair and eyes. Even more important, the jacket's padded shoulders and bulky weave adequately camouflaged her condition.

She studied herself in the full-length mirror and spread her fingers over her slight tummy bulge. When she'd last seen Nathan, her five-foot-seven frame had been lean as a greyhound. No wonder he'd commented on her increased weight. She could only hope he didn't guess at the reason for it.

After eating breakfast, she took the elevator downstairs to the first floor. When she and her father had bought the old nautical supply warehouse, they hired a crew to gut the interior and do extensive remodeling.

On the first floor, they set up their forensic investigative business with separate rooms for office, client conferences, and laboratory.

The second floor contained her father's one-bedroom apartment, her three-bedroom apartment, and one they eventually planned to rent out. The vacant third floor they used for storage. In a few years, Amy visualized it as being an ideal play area for her children.

She sobered. Last night, she'd been too exhausted to go through the hassle of breaking the news about the twins to her father. He hadn't made a secret about his opposition to the pregnancy, and had even counseled her early on about having an abortion. She shuddered at the thought of ridding herself of Nathan's children. The lives growing inside of her were the only thing that made her separation from Nathan bearable.

She plodded into the office. Because of the important evidence they kept on the premises, the laboratory entrance had a set of metal doors—one inside the other—both with numerical key-pad locks.

She punched in the code, opened the door, took several steps, fingered the next combination, and slipped inside. She adjusted her eyes to the bright fluorescent fixtures lighting the white-walled room. Around the area's outer perimeter ranged various machines used in analyzing physical evidence.

At a green Formica-covered counter, her father was hunched over a polarized-light microscope—just one of the half-a-dozen types strung out on either side of him.

"Morning, Dad."

He swung around, regarded her closely, and ran a hand over his bald pate. "Morning, kitten. How're you feeling?"

"Okay, I guess. Saw the specialist yesterday."

"Find out why your nausea has lasted so long?"

Amy jacked up her courage and plunged in. "He says it's not unusual for someone who's going to have twins."

His eyes widened. "Twins! Good God, Amy, have you taken leave of your senses? One baby is ridiculous. Two is impossible."

She braced her hands on her hips. "These are my babies." She thumped her chest. "Mine. I'll never abort them. Either accept that, or I'll move out so you won't be reminded of my loose morals."

B.J.'s eyes shot blue flame. "Dammit, Amy, get your head out of the clouds. How the hell will you be able to find a husband if you've got two kids?"

Amy raised her chin and met his fiery gaze. "I don't want a husband, Dad. I love Nathan."

He scrubbed his hand over his face. "With two kids as a daily reminder, you're not apt to forget him either."

"I don't want to forget him."

"Obviously." He sighed wearily. "I've been down that road. For your information, it is not a damned stroll in the park!"

Amy pressed her hand against her stomach. "I don't think you did too bad, Dad."

He drew his heavy brows together in a scowl. "Dammit, I just want you to have a normal life," he muttered. "Is anything wrong with that?"

"No, Dad. It just isn't going to be that way."

"So I see." He bent over the microscope again. "I'd like to tell that damn dream man of yours just what I think of him."

Amy let out her breath slow and easy. "You just might get that opportunity. Yesterday I had lunch with Nathan at the Maxfield Hotel."

B.J. spun around. "You what?"

"He was there attending a resort owner's conference."

B.J. thinned his lips to a hard line. "And you just *happened* to run into each other."

"We didn't plan it, Dad."

"So how's his marriage between friends going?"

"I have no idea." Amy jammed her hands into her jacket pockets. "Oh, and by the way, he'll be here this morning."

"Christ, what next." B.J.'s penetrating stare pinned her in place. "Are you going to tell him?"

Her expression grew hard. "No, and neither are you. If I know Nathan, he's only coming because he thinks he can help us out on the Nguyen case."

"Great pretext," B.J. said sarcastically. He slid off his stool and took hold of her shoulders. "Amy, if you're determined to have his children, he deserves to know."

She wrenched herself out of his grasp. "Why? He

doesn't want two more half-breed Blackthorns any more than you do."

"Whoa, girl." B.J. leveled a finger at her. "Their race isn't an issue here. Children need a mother *and* a father. And you damn well know it."

"We'll manage." She headed for the front office. "I'll let you know when Nathan arrives. And Dad"—she turned and regarded him sternly—"Behave."

The stack of paperwork had diminished by only a few sheets when the foyer door slammed and Nathan opened the office door. "Hi," he said as he ambled over to her desk.

She pressed her back against the chair and tried to appear casual. "You're out and about early."

A self-conscious grin lifted one corner of his mouth. "I know, I know. I couldn't wait to see . . . to get here."

Amy regarded him as if she'd never seen him before. Marriage had changed him. The Nathan she knew had kept his emotions hidden. Now there was a definite gleam of anticipation in his eyes. Was he here because . . . her world shifted on its axis and she curbed the thought. She had to guard against foolish hopes.

She lifted the phone receiver with an unsteady hand. "My father's in the lab. He'll want to hear your ideas about the case. That *is* why you're here, right?"

"Oh . . . of course," he said, then sat down abruptly. "I forgot about your father."

"Dad, can you come out here please?" she said into the receiver, set it back in place, and studied Nathan again.

He wore a white shirt, brown twill pants, and a brown leather jacket. His hair was several inches shorter than it had been the day before. "You got your hair cut," she said.

"It was time." He rested his ankle on his knee and centered his gaze on the heel of his western-style boot. "Wearing my hair that way was childish, anyhow."

"Oh, why do you say that?"

He turned his hand palm-up. "Daring people to question my Native American heritage." A muscle worked along his jaw. "I should have forgotten the half-breed taunts long ago."

"Wounds sometimes take a long time to heal."

The inner metal door of the lab klunked shut and moments later Amy's father strode into the office. His battle-ready countenance at the sight of Nathan propelled her across the room. She put a propitiatory arm around his rigid shoulders. "Dad, I'd like you to meet Nathan Blackthorn," she said as she led him over to where Nathan stood. "Nathan, this is my father, B.J. Prescott."

Nathan put out his hand. "I've heard a lot about you, Doctor."

"Oh?" B.J. ignored Nathan's proffered hand. "Like what?"

Amy winced. She should have known this was a bad idea.

Under B.J.'s cold scrutiny, Nathan's face tightened. "I keep up with what's going on in the investigative business. Habit, I guess." He shifted his attention to Amy for an instant and raised an eyebrow.

She returned his gaze with reassurance in her eyes.

"Well?" B.J. snapped and folded his arms. "Amy tells me you've come about the Nguyen case."

Nathan stared down at the older man for a full beat before he spoke. "I spent six months in Cambodia. Two with the hill tribes on the Thai border, two with the Hinayana Buddhist monks, and another two wandering the country."

She eyed her father. He knew how volatile the situation in Cambodia had been. Many of them hated the Americans for backing Pol Pot.

B.J. blinked owlishly but maintained his belligerent stance. "Doing what?"

"Gathering classified information. I speak Khmer, French, and Vietnamese. I might be able to reach people you and Amy cannot."

Amy caught her breath. In the last three minutes, she'd learned more about Nathan's role in the Special Forces than he'd told her in the weeks they had worked together. But she had no time to think of that now. Her father's expression was impenetrable.

She stretched her mouth into a smile. "We really appreciate your coming, Nathan." She gestured toward an open doorway behind her. "Let's go into the conference room."

She hooked her arm through B.J.'s and motioned for Nathan to preceede them. "Stop it," she said to her father under her breath.

"I'll do as I damn please," he muttered. "This is my business too."

She glared at him. "If you continue to be so rude, you'll be running it by yourself." When they were both seated in the conference room, Amy set two mugs from a side counter on the table.

She offered Nathan another reassuring smile. "I'll get some coffee." When she turned to head back to their small kitchen, he pushed back his chair and followed her.

"Let me help," he said eagerly.

"Well . . . if you insist." In the alcove, she switched

on the toaster oven to warm some oat bran muffins she'd baked earlier. "Sorry about Dad," she said. "He has an attitude problem this morning."

"I deserve it, and more . . . much more."

Amy took a black lacquer tray from a slot beneath the birch cabinets and placed it on the counter. "You don't, Nathan. You were honest with me. You told me you were engaged."

"No!" Nathan leaned down until his eyes were on a level with hers and touched his fingertip to her lips. "No, Amy. Not soon enough. We both know that. I should have stayed away from you."

She picked up a sponge and wiped the already spotless counter. "I'm glad you didn't," she said softly.

The air whistled out of Nathan's lungs as a bleak cast spread over his features. "Amy . . ."

The toaster bell dinged, breaking the intimate mood. "You still take your coffee black?" she asked.

At his nod, she took a ceramic bowl containing packets of sugar and cream substitute from the cupboard and smiled at him with her eyes. "I'm trying to keep Dad's weight and cholesterol down." She set out silverware and dessert plates, located a tub of margarine in the countertop refrigerator, and slid the muffins out of the toaster oven.

Nathan inhaled their aroma and the corners of his mouth twitched. "Cholesterol- and calorie-free?"

She grinned back. "Near as I could make them. If you'll carry the tray, we'll rejoin the fire-eating dragon."

In the birch-paneled conference room, B.J. sat at the head of the square table, writing progress notes in a manila folder. To her relief, he had distributed pencils and scratch pads. He had even made a copy of their current investigative report for Nathan.

After Amy initiated the discussion and got the men talking, she slipped away to the kitchen and returned with a glass of water and a piece of hard, dry toast for herself. She seated herself next to Nathan as though to remind her father that her loyalties were with the man beside her.

Nathan glanced up from the sheaf of papers he held. "The muffins are delicious. Don't you want one?"

"Uh . . ." Beads of perspiration broke out on her upper lip. "I . . . had mine already." When both men simply stared at her, she wished she'd put on more makeup, made herself look less pale. Nathan's probing gaze became skeptical; B.J.'s anxious and concerned.

She took a quick gulp of water. "Dad, would you give us a brief review of your postmortem?"

Upon hearing the stress she'd put on the word *us*, B.J. flung her a caustic look and passed around five-by-seven-inch colored pictures of the body. "The victim had lip and scalp lacerations. There were numerous contusions on her face and body. Most of the knife wounds on her throat and breasts are superficial. The fatal stab wound entered between the fifth and sixth rib. The blade severed the heart's left coronary artery and penetrated the left ventricle."

"She'd have bled out pretty fast," Amy said.

Nathan touched Amy's arm. "Her husband said she was still alive when he found her, right?"

"Uh-huh."

"Then either the killer had just left, or your friend is lying."

Amy raised her chin, steadied her gaze. "He's not."

Nathan's expression softened. "You can't be sure of that, Amy. He's a doctor. Whoever killed her knew where to stab her so it would be fatal."

B.J. scowled and cleared his throat. "She had some fairly large pieces of tissue under her fingernails."

Amy brightened. "Enough for a DNA?"

"I asked for a polymerase chain reaction."

"Good." She noticed Nathan's puzzled frown. "A PCR test provides the highest degree of DNA identification available."

"I see." Nathan turned to B.J. "Was she raped?"

"Yes, savagely. And she had what appears to be electrical burns on her genitalia."

A muscle twitched in Nathan's jaw. "Have you ever seen anything like that before?"

"Not in the twenty years I've been a medical examiner," B.J. said.

Amy shuddered. "I've seen some terrible sexual assault cases, but never anything like that."

"The victim also had denuded areas of skin on her wrists and ankles."

"Was she tied up?" Nathan asked.

"I found cotton fibers."

Amy frowned. "I wonder why neither Cam nor the sheriff mentioned that." She made a note on her scratch pad. "What kind of restraint?"

"Rope. I called Boyce," B.J. said. "He says she wasn't bound when he arrived and no rope was taken from the scene."

"Hah! After what I've seen of him, that doesn't mean a whole lot. What did you learn about the stab wounds?"

B.J. rose, took an X-ray from a brown envelope, slid it under the clip on the fluorescent view box, and flipped the switch. Amy and Nathan gathered around him.

B.J. pointed to an elongated white area on the black

film. "Evidently her assailant twisted the knife in the wound. The barium sulfate doesn't give a clear outline."

"Any bruises around the entrance wound?" Amy asked.

"Yes."

"So the knife went in to the hilt." She picked up a ruler and placed it on the outline of the barium. "Blade is approximately seven inches long."

"And the entrance wound measured one inch," B.J. said.

"Okay, we've got the dimensions of the weapon." She folded her arms and continued to stare at the film. "What else do we know about it?"

"Something damned peculiar." B.J. frowned and tugged at his beard. "The tissues of the heart wall look shredded."

"Probably a double-edged dagger with a saw edge on the back," Nathan murmured, almost to himself.

B.J., his lips compressed into a thin line, turned to face him. "How do you know?"

Nathan didn't meet his gaze. "I've seen a few."

Amy recalled the knife he'd held against her throat the night they met. In his type of work, she suspected he may have needed to know a great deal about weapons of all kinds. "Did the superficial wounds on the body reveal anything?"

B.J. removed the X-ray and substituted another. "I used the melted Wood's metal as you suggested." He beamed at Amy. "Look what I got."

Amy returned his grin. "It's about time we got something solid." Although only half an inch of the knife image showed, it was enough. It was evident that the weapon used in the murder had a tiny nick near the tip.

B.J. shut off the viewer and they once again took their seats.

Amy jotted down some points she wanted to remember, then asked, "Anything interesting on the vacuum filters from the Nguyen house?"

"Something a bit odd. I found traces of magnesium carbonate in the areas where Mai and her assailant struggled."

Amy recorded the substance in her notes. "In the kitchen?"

"Kitchen and bedroom."

"Hmmm," she said and scribbled some more. "Could be a crushed antacid tablet or a laxative of some sort, I guess."

"Weight lifters use it," Nathan said. He put down the investigation notes he'd been reading. "I just bought some for the exercise room at the lodge."

B.J. gazed at him for a moment, sighed, and ran a hand over his face. "Amy, do you know if Cam lifts weights?"

5

Wheeler was situated only thirty-five miles from Ursa Bay. Yet today, with scowling, gunmetal clouds hanging above the tops of the Douglas firs and drifting fog shrouding the landscape, the distance seemed much greater.

Amy sat on the seat of Nathan's rental car, her back straight, her hands knotted in her lap. During the planning of the trip out to the Nguyen house, she'd foolishly offered to ride with Nathan to show him the way. B.J. had given her one of his who-do-you-think-you're-kidding looks. After that, she refused to change her mind even though she knew her emotions would take a battering.

Since B.J. had a business appointment, he had gone on ahead. He intended to meet them at a park-and-ride lot in Wheeler. He advised Nathan to leave his car at the lot and pick it up later. Although Sheriff Boyce had given them permission to reenter the Nguyen house, Amy and B.J. both thought it wise not to broadcast Nathan's involvement in the case.

Amy jumped as a loaded logging truck honked at them and swooshed by, showering their car with bits of fir bark.

Nathan frowned at the truck's winking taillights. "Do

you have any pictures of Pran and the Nguyens aside
from the ones you've loaned me?"

"A number of Cam and Mai. But only the one of
Chantou Pran. I can have a copy made, if you think it's
important."

"It could be." Nathan seemed lost in thought for a
moment, then said, "The woman's electrical burns both-
ers me."

Amy's mind clenched, shutting out images of Mai's
terrible ordeal—dwelling on it did no good and only
muddled her thinking.

Nathan flipped on his signal. Tires hissing on wet asphalt, he swept past a slow-moving car and returned to
the right-hand lane. "An insanely jealous man could be
capable of such a thing." He threaded the car over a nar-
row, steel girder bridge spanning a river. Below them, a
torrent of brown water leaped and churned, throwing
white spume onto great, sheer-sided rocks. "But that
type of sadism smacks of something much more sinister
than a jealous rage."

"Like what?"

He glanced at her with a worried expression. "I
would rather not say just now. "It's only a hunch."

She regarded him carefully, but decided against press-
ing him. Instead, she wrapped her voluminous raincoat
around her and stared into space.

As the miles rolled by, she became increasingly conscious of Nathan's nearness, the faint, familiar odor of
soap and shaving cream. From time to time, she felt him
glance at her, but she did not return his looks.

Finally, he switched on the radio. Strains of a Patsy
Cline love ballad filled the car. *Oh, please, not that
song,* she thought. She squeezed her eyes shut, yet
couldn't hold back the flood of memories the melody

awakened. The same song filling a cabin in the woods, firelight flickering on their bodies as they made love . . .

Suddenly Nathan braked, pulled to the side of the road, and stopped the car. "Amy."

The timbre of his voice drew her gaze upward. Her eyes met his and desire surged through her.

"Amy . . ." he whispered. "I dream of you." He leaned closer and tilted her chin. "Could I—"

She blinked and shook herself as if coming out of a trance. "Don't . . . Nathan." She bent her head. "Please don't." She stared fixedly at her hands. The words of the song intensified the ache inside her. She reached out to switch off the radio, but Nathan beat her to it.

"I'm sorry." He gripped the steering wheel. "I told myself I only wanted to help you. That I would not let this happen."

"It's my fault."

"No, it's not." He pounded the wheel with his fists. "I knew. In my heart, I knew. I couldn't see you again without . . . without . . ."

"Nathan, please. I think it's best if we just get going. Don't you?"

He turned, smiled at her sadly, and nodded, starting up the car and pulling back onto the road.

The car dipped into a rocky ravine darkened by pendulous fir and cedar boughs. The purple-shadowed forest reminded her of the hikes she and Nathan took while searching for her friend, Simon.

"Do you ever see Kittredge?"

Amy flung him a startled look. Had he read her thoughts? "Almost every week. He's staying at Dad's house on Lomitas Island."

"I see." Nathan veered through the last switchback,

came out on the crest of a hill, and headed down into a wide, flat valley. "Still working for Global News?"

She shook her head. "He's taken a leave of absence to write a book." She recalled their last meeting. "Weekends, we build a fire on the beach and talk half the night." She stretched her mouth into a caricature of a smile. "It's a good thing our place is secluded. The arguments we have would wake the neighbors."

Stony-faced, he peered out the window at a paint-peeled barn. "So you're still mothering him."

She regarded him for a long moment. "Sometimes, I just need someone I can talk to." She pointed ahead. "The lot where we're meeting Dad is on the right."

Nathan parked the car near B.J.'s van and cut the motor. "You can always reach me at the lodge, you know, or at Dr. Chamber's cabin."

She stared at him, anger heating her cheeks. "You and your wife are living in the cabin where I stayed?" *Where they'd met and talked and made love . . .*

"Angela kept her apartment in Orofino. She teaches second grade." He reached into the backseat and lifted out a large duffel bag. "I go home weekends."

Amy steadied the trembling inside her. "Why are you staying at the cabin?"

"It's the only place I can sleep," he said simply, then got out of the car and closed the door.

She took a second to pull herself together. *The only place he could sleep.* Did that mean he could only find peace in the bed in which *she'd* slept?

She trudged over to the van. B.J. had already situated Nathan on an overturned box in the rear. On either side of him ranged built-in compartments holding forensic supplies. A collapsible gurney slid into a metal slot. Light and camera tripods lay in a tangle held in place by both her and B.J.'s medical bags and their respective forensic kits.

She hoisted herself into the black vinyl bucket seat next to her father and without thinking let out a sigh. "Let's go."

B.J. gave her a long, level look. "You okay?"

She managed a weak smile. "Of course. I'm strong as an elephant and twice as healthy."

"Like hell you are." He maneuvered the van onto the potholed roadway and a stiff silence settled around them.

Amy swung around to Nathan. "Wheeler was founded in 1910," she said, hoping to lessen the tension. "The town nearly died before the Southeast Asian families moved in and leased these places."

She gestured to weathered two-story houses bordering the street. Instead of lawns, long rows of rich, black, cultivated earth bracketed each building. "The tenants raise flowers for the florist trade. Make use of every inch of soil.

"The whole valley is a patchwork of glowing color during spring, summer, and fall. Hundreds of people come." She kept up her rambling, tour-guide patter until Nathan rested his hand lightly on her shoulder. Amy took the hint and subsided.

The street widened, became better paved as shops crowded out the houses. A blue sports car with a middle-aged man at the wheel darted out of a side street and B.J. slammed on his brakes. "Stupid idiot ran a stop sign."

"Patience, Dad." She caught a glimmer of amusement in Nathan's glance. "As you can see, Nathan, some of the Caucasian locals have gotten rich off the tourists."

"Do Kampucheans work in any of the stores?"

"Mostly in the restaurants, curio shops, and vegetable and flower markets at the other end of town."

"Does Wheeler have an athletic club?"

"I don't know. Do you, Dad?"

"Nope."

"I'll check." Nathan made a note on a piece of paper.

B.J. turned at a red brick courthouse and cruised through a residential area until the houses thinned out and they came to a sign that said, PRAN'S LANDSCAPE GARDENS. They drove down a densely wooded lane to a graveled parking area.

Broad overhangs with uplifted gables like those found in Cambodian temples decorated the gently pitched roof of the Nguyen house. Carved cedar pillars supported a front porch flanked by vine-covered lattice work.

B.J. pulled up beside a separate building that appeared to be a combined equipment shed, garage, and workroom. "Got the key, kitten?"

Nathan slid open the back door of the van. "Doctor, do you mind if I have a look inside first?"

B.J. shrugged. "How long do you need?"

"Ten minutes ought to do it."

Amy handed him the key Cam's attorney had sent by messenger. "Let us know when you're ready," she said.

B.J. scowled and slumped down in his seat. "What the hell does he think he can find that we didn't?"

"You might be surprised. His grandfather taught him remarkable skills, and the government picked up where he left off."

She got out of the van and followed thyme-fringed stepping stones to a hedged-in plot. Crushed herbs assailing her nostrils, she opened a wrought-iron gate and strolled through Mai's private garden.

Mai's father had clipped hemlock and boxwood into topiary urns, balls, cubes, and castles. He'd shaped and sheared yew into scores of animals—peacocks, rabbits, squirrels, even a dragon. He must have been a devoted father to have spent so much time on his daughter's garden when he had a landscape business to run, Amy thought.

Her throat constricted as she recalled Mai and Cam standing beside the castle and dragon topiary during their wedding ceremony.

She gazed through drifting veils of fog at endless rows of trees and shrubs flanked by long, glass-enclosed greenhouses. After a moment, she emitted a long sigh. Now, both Mai and her father were dead.

When she heard Nathan's voice, she hurried back through the gate and joined the men beneath the covered patio at the rear of the house.

B.J. stood with his hands in the pockets of his red nylon jacket. "So, what's the verdict?" Wind stirred long, suspended lengths of chimes on the porch. Their deep bell tones added a grave note to her father's words.

Nathan propped his shoulder against a black wrought-iron support. "Do either of the Nguyens smoke?"

"Not to my knowledge," Amy answered. "Why?"

"Someone who was in the house did. How about the sheriff?"

B.J. focused on a crack in the smooth, pink-concrete pathway. "Never saw him with a cigarette."

"Whoever it is smokes Djarum or Samporena cigarettes. They smell like incense."

B.J. bristled. "Impossible. We would have noticed such a thing."

Nathan strode to the back door and swung it open. "See for yourselves." He stood to one side and let them file through ahead of him.

Amy took one look at the kitchen and gasped. "Somebody's been here."

Cornflakes crackled under B.J.'s shoes. "Jesus, they trashed the place."

Nathan glanced from Amy to her father. "It wasn't like this when you did your initial investigation?"

Amy shook her head. "It showed signs of a struggle, but nothing like this."

B.J. stepped carefully around spilled sugar and flour, slipped on rice grains, and caught hold of a chair. "What a god-awful mess. Must have been hooligans."

"I don't think so."

B.J. swung around and glared at Nathan. "Why not?"

"Everything's been put through a sieve. They dumped the rest into pots and pans."

Amy analyzed the scene. Cupboard doors gaped, broken glass littered the countertop. The contents of overturned drawers mounded on the floor. A mess to be true, but an orderly mess all the same. "Someone's looking for something." She turned to Nathan. "Right?"

"Something small, is my guess. They pried the baseboards and electrical outlets off in the other rooms." He hooked his thumbs in the back pockets of his pants and said quietly, "Smell the cigarette smoke?"

B.J. eyed him steadily. "Yes." He turned his back. "I'll take this room, Amy. You go through the others and see if we should reprocess them. Then we'd better contact the sheriff."

Nathan shifted from one foot to the other. "If it's all right with you, I'd like to look around outside."

"I've already gone over the grounds around the house." B.J. made a sweeping motion with his hand. "But, sure, go do whatever you want to do." His tone was less than gracious.

Nathan stiffened and looked away. Amy scowled at

her father, moved to Nathan's side and put her hand on his arm. "See you in a little while."

His expression softened slightly and he nodded.

After Nathan left, Amy followed the trail of incense-scented cigarette smoke into the living room. A sofa and two chairs rested on their backs, their white satin coverings slashed, their padding pulled out.

Beside a six-foot-tall feather palm, the brass-hinged doors of a chest hung open. A raw cigarette burn marred the black lacquered top. Gray ash dotted the oak flooring beneath the chest's carved feet.

Amy clenched her teeth. The bastard desecrated Mai's body, then he savaged her house. Rigid with anger, she marched into the study. Books lay everywhere, each with its spine slit.

She picked up a dog-eared children's book illustrated with crude pen and ink drawings. Thinking it might be a keepsake of Mai's, Amy slid the slim volume into her pocket to give to Cam, and moved on to inspect the bathroom.

Lotions, creams, pills, and bath crystals filled the sink to overflowing. Discarded containers cluttered the countertop and floor. Amy swore under her breath and continued her survey.

In the master bedroom, piles of mattress stuffing dotted the parquet floor. An intricately made screen slumped in a corner, its bamboo sections split open like a gutted fish. What was it that would drive anyone to such wanton destruction? she wondered.

"Amy," Nathan said, startling her out of her reverie. She turned as he made his way toward her, his boot heels thudding on bare flooring. As he always did when following a trail, he kept to the periphery, to avoid walking where others might have walked. "I found something I think you and your father should see."

Laura Featherston

6

"I've got plenty to do right here," B.J. said irritably when Amy asked him to accompany her and Nathan outside. "Look at this." He held up a shard of glass tipped with what looked like blood, dropped it into an evidence bag, and scribbled an I.D. on the fluorescent red label.

"It'll keep Dad, Nathan's found something."

"Blast it! You know I don't like other people messing around in my case," B.J. said, deliberately ignoring Nathan, who stood in the doorway behind him.

Nathan's nostrils flared, but he gave no other indication he'd heard the older man.

Amy's patience snapped. "What case? We hardly have a case at this point."

B.J. looked up, startled by her tone. "All right, all right. Don't get so upset." He flipped up the gray hood of his magnified viewer and peered at Nathan. "Let's see what you've got."

"Wait until I get my camera and forensic kit," Amy said as she started for the door.

"How do you know you'll need them?"

She turned and gave a hint of a grin. "I know Nathan."

Nathan suddenly brightened. "I'll get your gear."

B.J. fidgeted as he and Amy waited for him by the back step. "This cowboy of yours is getting on my nerves," he said.

"You might try giving him half a chance."

"Why? I don't owe him anything."

"He's my friend."

"Hah! Some friend."

They quieted as Nathan hastened from the red cinder driveway and handed Amy her camera. "Start over here." Carrying her forensic kit and a long, thin piece of doweling he'd picked up somewhere, he skirted the patio and squatted down at the far edge. Amy and B.J. moved closer.

Nathan tapped his improvised pointer on the pink concrete. "Get down on all fours and sight across."

Amy and B.J. did as he instructed. "You referring to those small clumps of mud on the concrete?" she asked.

"Uh-huh."

B.J. inched forward. "Okay to get closer?"

When Nathan nodded, B.J. flipped down his magnified viewer and advanced slowly. "They form a kind of pattern."

"Yes, he left his flip-flops there."

"Thongs? In January? Hell, the man would have to be nuts."

"Most Southeast Asians wear *shek choeung phtoat* from the time they can walk. They're cheap and more practical than shoes."

Nathan stood and gestured to a grove of evergreens approximately a hundred yards away. "He came from that direction. And he's been here twice. The first time was about five days ago."

Amy drew in her breath. "When Mai was killed."

Nathan nodded. "He came back again last night."

B.J. stubbornly pushed out his lip and stood. "How do you know?"

Nathan jerked his head. "Follow me." He picked up Amy's kit and walked along in a bent, tracking stance for several yards before hunkering down again. "Things grow in harmony with their surroundings," he said solemnly. "If they do not, there is a reason for it."

He touched an area of slender green spears of grass that were bent at a forty-five-degree angle. "These were disturbed about five hours ago. Now look at those over there"—he held his stick over blades with a barely perceptible bend—"Similar vegetation recover their normal position at the same rate." He regarded B.J. with a half smile. "If the weather has not changed."

B.J. folded his arms. "That it?"

"Not quite." Nathan rose and headed toward the woods.

Her shoes now soggy, Amy trotted along at his side. "You followed that practically invisible trail all this way?"

He wagged his head. "Actually, I started at the woods and worked backwards."

Amy knotted her brows. "Why there?"

"I've been in this guy's shoes." He chuckled. "Make that thongs. When you're on a stakeout in terrain like this, you find the tallest tree."

With his shoulder, he held aside pendulous cedar branches. Motioning Amy and B.J. into a rosin-scented arbor, he pointed upward. "Our man used that tree." Twenty feet away stood a Douglas fir with wisps of mist coiling lazily around its corky-barked trunk.

"This is more than I could possibly have hoped for." Amy followed Nathan on his roundabout route, her feet sinking into layers of moist, black, decaying needles.

He stopped about ten feet from the towering fir. "He came here over a period of several weeks."

Twigs snapping underfoot, B.J. waded through a patch of leathery-leafed salal. "And how did you determine that?" he asked.

"I just know." Nathan's quick glance begged Amy's forgiveness, for his sharp tone. He set down the forensic bag, wrapped his arm around a sapling, and leaned far out. "Notice these?" He held his stick over something at the base of the tree.

Amy found a patch of club moss, got down on all fours, and stared into the gloom beneath the sweeping branches. Finally, her eyes focused in on Nathan's find. "Cigarillo butts."

"Djarum. They're manufactured in Indonesia." He moved his pointer a couple of feet. "Can you see the cellophane? It's a slightly heavier variety than ours." He touched a clump of dried sword ferns. "The empty packs are stuffed under here."

Amy thought of the valuable DNA information the saliva-dampened cigarettes might yield. "You certainly found a treasure trove."

She swung around to B.J.. "This, along with the blood you found, could prove decisive."

"Doesn't prove he's the murderer."

"No?" Nathan stomped through a thicket of red alder. He stopped near a stump, teased aside rotted wood with his piece of doweling, and exposed two flat metal prongs embedded in black rubber. "That convince you?"

"Jesus Christ, an electrical cord! I gotta get more light in here!" B.J. spun around and bolted back the way they'd come. Suddenly he stopped and yelled back, "Don't touch a thing. Not a thing, hear?"

Nathan lowered himself onto a fallen log. "Does he ever let up?"

When Amy smiled, Nathan flung her a sour look. "Something funny?"

"I just figured out what's eating him."

"Fine. I'm glad *you* know."

Any uncapped her camera and snapped a picture of the protruding electrical plug. "He started out being angry because he thought you'd hurt me." She returned to the big fir and focused in on the cigarette butts. "Now, his nose is out of joint because he realizes your knowledge is on a par with his."

"Great. That puts me on his list."

She laughed out loud and triggered the camera. "You two are very much alike."

"Thanks, just what I wanted to hear."

She ambled over to where he sat. "I meant it as a compliment. I happen to think my dad is a very special guy."

Nathan spread his hands. "And you think *I* am, after all I've done to you?"

"You didn't set out to hurt me, Nathan. I don't blame you for what happened between us."

His expression softened as he brushed his knuckle across her cheek. "Kitten," he said slowly, as if getting the feel of the name. "Nice. I like it." He managed a wry smile. "At least your father got that right." He studied the tips of his muddy boots, then met her gaze once more. "You are a very special person, too."

Not hardly, Amy thought. A special person would be honest and aboveboard and not yearn for a man who belonged to another woman. She swallowed. "Maybe. Maybe not." When she ran her tongue over her dry lips, she saw a flame kindle in Nathan's eyes. "I'd better get busy." She smiled at him. "Mind if I get a picture of you?" In the difficult months ahead, she'd need one.

"Not if you'll let me take some of you."

Amy took photographs of the vicinity, then revisited the lookout tree. Kneeling on the forest duff and inhaling the damp mushroom odors, she got several close-ups of the site. Finally, the knees of her wool slacks sodden, she struggled to her feet.

She felt Nathan's presence, and shivered when he came up behind her and drew her back against him. "I've missed you so much."

I shouldn't let him do this. A heartbeat passed, then another and another as she held herself perfectly still, afraid if she made the slightest movement, he'd let go of her.

Nathan buried his face in the hollow of her neck and breathed in. "Oh, Amy girl."

They remained that way for several moments, until a crashing of underbrush heralded B.J.'s return. Nathan sighed and moved away from her before her father caught sight of them. "I have something else to show you."

He took her hand and led her around to the back side of the big Douglas fir. A fresh scar exposed tan and dark brown inner bark. Below lay bits of shavings and whittled sticks.

Amy gripped his hand hard. "Does it mean anything? Do you think he did it to pass the time?"

"Might have."

"If it's the same knife he used to kill Mai, we just might get lucky and find a tie-in." As she started to turn away, something caught her eye in the litter at the tree's base. "What's that?"

"Where?"

She snatched up a twig, turned over a brownish, fir-needle-covered blob, and regarded it intently. "A piece of candy." She wheeled around and grabbed his jacket front. "Caramel candy with tooth marks." She gave an excited laugh. "That'll be a challenge." She sobered and stared up at him. "Oh, Nathan. This will help us so much. Without you, we might never have discovered any of this."

He flushed and put his arm around her. "I'm so glad I can help you. I—" Suddenly, B.J.'s bellow cut him off.

"Amy! Where the hell are you?"

"Coming!" Amy yelled. She grinned at Nathan. "Subtle, he ain't."

"That's okay. I've got to go make some preparations. Mind if I use the laundry sink and mirror in the garage?"

She looked at him questioningly, then shrugged. "Fine with me."

"When she reached B.J., he was setting up battery-powered torches to better view the scene. "Ran onto a couple of interesting items on the other side of the tree," she said.

"Did you get pictures?"

"Enough for the first stage."

"Good. Get out the camcorder and document every move we make. I don't want any loopholes."

"Will do." Removing small evidence bags from her kit, she began to label them. "Did you call the sheriff?"

"Yeah, he says he'll stop by when he can get away." B.J. snorted derisively. "Probably caught him in the middle of a hot pinochle game." He inspected the floor of the area through his magnifier. "Damn this furry green stuff."

"It's moss, Dad. *Leucolepis menziesii.*"

"Just what I need, another expert," B.J. said. He bent to concentrate once more. "Can't make out anything you'd call a footprint. Wish to hell this guy had worn shoes." He bent down farther. "Tweezers," he said, and Amy slapped the requested item into his hand. "Bag." She held the sack open while he dropped in a cigarette butt.

"Ah," he said, drawing the word out with obvious satisfaction. "I see how Nathan knew the murderer had come here over a period of time. The butts tell a story."

Amy smiled to herself. She knew Nathan would have taken many elements into consideration—just as she or B.J. would have—before making such a remark. "From the looks of this, Mai was right in thinking someone was spying on her. He may have even made his presence known, just to intimidate her."

"Wouldn't be a bit surprised." He lay a telescoping platform he'd invented over intervening space and inched toward the tree. With slow, painstaking exactness, B.J. gathered and packaged each piece of evidence while she took turns using the still camera and the camcorder.

Nearly an hour passed before they reached the rotted stump and started to unearth the electrical cord. "Well I'll be damned," B.J. said as he carefully lifted a chunk of wood and set it aside. "Look at that." Crammed in behind the cord lay four short lengths of white cotton rope. He cleared his throat. "Seems as if your Nathan knows a thing or two after all."

Amy smiled, but remained silent.

Finally, they gathered their materials and equipment and made their way out of the grove. As they neared the house, a rotund man in a black suit emerged from the garage and came toward them.

He stopped several yards away, pressed his palms together and brought them humbly in toward his body.

"Doctor Prescott, I am Khieu Ngor. Chantou Pran's nephew."

B.J. stared hard at the man for a moment before uttering, "Holy Jesus. It's you."

Although Amy had seen Nathan in disguise before, the transformation still amazed and rather frightened her. Each time, she felt as if the man she knew had been usurped by another. Now, by some means or other he gave the appearance of having shortened his height, put on weight, and aged. His naturally slanted eyes fit his assumed part, but he'd partially concealed them with round, steel-rimmed glasses.

Nathan smiled. "Think I'll pass?" Even his voice sounded different.

She shivered. "You carrying your gun?"

"I don't think I'll need it."

B.J. cleared his throat. "We're dealing with a violent man. You could be walking into a dangerous situation."

"I've been there before." A siren shrilled in the distance. "I had better get going. I'll come by your office later."

"Don't you need a ride?" Amy asked.

"No," he said. "It's best I go on foot. We shouldn't be seen together, and besides, I'll learn more this way."

Amy fought down an urge to plead with him not to go. "Be careful."

He grinned, a strange toothy smile that didn't resemble his own at all. Amy saw that he'd already vanished into his new persona.

Nathan raised his hand in farewell and headed off toward the woods.

7

In the Nguyens' master bedroom, B.J. dusted finely grained gray powder onto a bamboo screen. When it swayed, Sheriff Boyce reached out to steady it. "Hands off!" B.J. snapped.

The stocky man yanked his hand back. "Kee-*rist*, Prescott, you'd think this was some damned major crime scene or something."

B.J. straightened. "And just what the hell do *you* think it is? Someone murdered Mai Nguyen in this house. And then returned, looking for something."

Sheriff Boyce's bulbous nose reddened. "Waste of time. Just a bunch of kids out to make some mischief."

Amy lifted her camel-hair dusting brush and regarded the man with annoyance. "Kids would have left fingerprints everywhere," she said, turning back to dust the bureau drawers.

B.J. glanced up from his work. "And I haven't found any that weren't here before."

"Kids go to the movies. They know the score."

B.J. expelled his breath noisily. "How would they have gotten in? We didn't find any broken windows or doors."

"So"—Deputy Pierce straightened his hat—"What's your theory?"

B.J. fixed him with a hard-eyed stare. "The person who murdered Mrs. Nguyen probably stole a key the night he murdered her."

"That's a laugh," Sheriff Boyce said. "Since when doesn't a husband have a key to his own house?"

"Ah, come off it, Sheriff." Amy braced her fists on her hips. "You saw the evidence we gathered in the woods. What's it take to convince you there's more going on here than what you thought?"

Sheriff Boyce jutted out his square chin. "You got no proof linking that cache in the woods to what happened in this house." He jerked his head at his deputy. "Come on, Duane. We got more important things to do than dusting cabinets."

By the time Amy and her father finished their work and returned to Ursa Bay, Amy felt as exhausted as if she'd climbed a mountain. Nevertheless, she trudged into the lab and began organizing the physical evidence they'd collected.

Several of the cigarette butts they arranged to send out for a polymerase chain reaction; others they'd analyze themselves. She made a silent prayer that the man who killed Mai secreted ABO antigens. If he didn't, they'd have to take another route.

She wrote a note to their forensic odontology consultant requesting an impression of the teeth marks in the piece of caramel candy they'd found, and put the package in the outgoing mail. With luck, the specialist would be able to tell them something about the perpetrator's facial contours.

Tomorrow, B.J. intended to return to the stakeout area with a saw and wood chisel to extract the whittled bark. If the marks revealed striations or other anomalies that matched with the barium sulfate X-rays taken of the victim's wound, they would have a definite tie-in.

While she worked, B.J. busied himself in another part of the lab. He wanted to run tests on droplets of dried blood he'd found on the countertops in the Nguyens' kitchen and bathroom.

At 5:00 P.M., the buzzer on the office's front door sounded. Amy met Nathan there, and saw that somewhere during his return, he'd gotten rid of his disguise. He tossed his leather jacket on the brown tweed settee and folded up his shirtsleeve cuffs, turning to regard her with a soft expression.

She beamed at him. "You're back safe and sound."

"Yep." He took a long white box from underneath his jacket. "These are for you."

She gave him a puzzled glance. "What for?"

"Because I've never given you anything." A bleak expression came over his face. "Nothing at all."

She took the box and gazed up at him. "You saved my life . . . *twice.*"

He shrugged. "Anybody could have done the same."

"That's not true." She set the box on the desk, lifted the lid, and caught her breath. "Red roses! Oh, Nathan, no one's ever given me flowers."

He moved closer. "No one?"

She shook her head. "I guess I'm not the type of woman men give gifts to."

He narrowed the space between them. "They were blind. You should have rings and necklaces and soft pink dresses . . ." His eyes met hers. "And lacy pink underthings."

She flushed. The last time they'd been together, she'd worn a pink skirt and blouse with matching lingerie. "Thank you. The roses are lovely." She blinked and swallowed hard. "I'll make them last."

He stood only inches from her, their bodies close but not touching. "Amy, I wish—" At the sound of the inner lab door clanking open, he stopped and stepped away from her.

She smiled apologetically. "My father will want to hear what you found out. Meet you in the conference room?" When he nodded, she whisked the roses into the kitchen and put them in a place where B.J. would be unlikely to find them. She didn't want him asking questions.

A few minutes later, they all gathered around the table in the conference room. She sat beside Nathan, as she had that morning.

"I covered all the Cambodian businesses," Nathan said, looking from Amy to her father. "Had lunch at the restaurant, made purchases at the curio, vegetable, and flower shops." He lifted two brown paper bags onto the table. One bulged with fruit, the other with vegetables. "Hope you can use this stuff."

Amy glimpsed an enormous head of broccoli and smiled. Her father hated broccoli. "I'm sure we will. Did you learn anything?"

Nathan drew his heavy brows together. "Nothing definite." His frown deepened. "Everywhere I went, I felt a puzzling undercurrent."

B.J. closed his file folder and clicked his ballpoint pen. "Might have known it. Didn't expect 'em to talk to a stranger."

Amy ignored his remark. "Did they say anything about Mai or her father?"

"Most knew and liked them. Odd, though ... questions about Pran's background ended the conversation." He took out a tiny roll of film and laid it on the table. "I carried a hidden camera and took pictures of everyone I talked to." He turned to Amy. "I'd like to keep the snapshot you gave me of Pran. I'll make a copy and return the original. I still have some contacts in Cambodia. I have a strange feeling ..."

Amy waited for him to continue. When he didn't, she asked, "Did you find a gym?"

Nathan took a folder from his jacket pocket and laid it in front of her. "Out of disguise, I went to Fenwick's Athletic Center. Played some handball. Worked out in the weight room. They have three Caucasian and two Asian employees." He handed B.J. a slip of paper. "I took the license numbers of the cars in the employee's lot."

B.J. stood up. "Anything else?"

Nathan wagged his head. "Nothing that I can put my finger on right now."

B.J. refiled the folder and dragged his easel and a huge pad of newsprint out of a corner. "Let's get some thoughts on paper." He uncapped a black felt pen. "What do we know about the suspect?"

"Judging from his stride and footprint impression, he's about five-foot-eight and weighs 130 to 135 pounds," Nathan said.

"He could be a Southeast Asian," Amy said.

Nathan sat forward. "He may lift weights."

Amy jotted a few lines in her black notebook. "I'll talk to Cam about that tomorrow."

"Also ask him which province Mai and her father came from," Nathan said, making a note to himself on his own scratch pad.

"Is that significant?" Amy asked.

"Could be. Somebody in that household has something someone wants badly enough to torture and kill for."

For a brief moment, she considered telling the two men about the blue pickup that had followed her from Wheeler. But she decided against it. It wasn't necessarily related to the case, she reasoned.

B.J. capped his pen and looked from one to the other. "That it?" When both she and Nathan nodded, he lay his pen in the grooved ledge of the easel and made eye contact with Amy. "Gotta go to a meeting, kitten. Be home around eleven."

"You get anything on that blood?"

"Oh yeah, I damn near forgot." He snatched up the felt pen again. "Type AB, Rh-negative. I'll do a PGM later. Got a Y-factor on the chromosome comp. The house wrecker is definitely a man."

"Hey, that's terrific, Dad." Amy got to her feet and hugged him. "Sure narrows the odds."

B.J. patted her back, shook himself loose, marched over to Nathan, and stuck out his hand. "Thanks."

With a look of surprise, Nathan shook the proffered hand. "I didn't accomplish much."

"You gave us the nudge we needed." B.J. swung around to Amy. "Get some rest," he said meaningfully.

"Is type AB blood rare?" Nathan asked after B.J. had gone.

Amy reseated herself beside him. "Only about six percent of the population has it." She frowned. "But nothing we've found today will be of any value if we don't come up with a suspect."

"Wish I could do more." Nathan set his elbows on the

table, interlaced his long, slender fingers, and rested his forehead against them.

Amy waited a long moment before asking what she knew she had to have the answer to. "Why did you come here today?"

He let out his breath. "Oh, Amy. Six years ago I left home because my father called me an arrogant fool. I traveled halfway around the world, and I am still an arrogant fool." He nodded his head in silent condemnation. "What gave me the right to think I knew what was best for you," or for Angela? I loused up your life and hers too."

She longed to put her arms around him; instead she reached over and began to rub his back. "I'll survive."

He leaned into her hand. "I'm not sure Angela and I will. I thought I could forget you. I didn't."

Amy continued to lightly massage his back; gradually his muscles relaxed under her touch.

His head rested once more on his folded hands. "Night after night, I run, trying to wear myself out so that I can sleep. But when I do, you're there in my dreams. I'm afraid I'll say your name . . . maybe I already have. Maybe that's why—"

"Shh, things will get better after . . ." Her voice faltered. "After you have children." But even while she said the words, she rejected the thought. The thought of him having children with anyone but her.

"I doubt that will ever happen." He ran a hand over his face wearily. "We don't . . . she can't . . ." He groaned. "I've really messed up our lives."

She swallowed into a dry throat and tried a different tack. "What you feel for me is only sexual attraction. You'll forget."

He twisted around and stared at her. "Have *you* forgotten?" When she didn't answer, he took her face in his hands. "Have you, Amy?"

She couldn't escape his fierce gaze, and knew he'd know if she lied. Her throat tightened and a fine trembling began inside her.

"Amy?"

The softness of his voice undid her. "No, I haven't forgotten."

"Are you speaking for your body or your heart?"

The trembling progressed to her legs and she pressed her hands against her knees. "I can't answer that, Nathan."

He flinched. "I *need* to know."

"My heart." A tear wet her cheek. She wiped it away with her fingers and raised her chin. "But I could be wrong. I thought I loved Mitch when I married him." She regretted the words as soon as she saw his expression. He knew what a mistake her first husband had turned out to be.

Nathan brought his chair closer and enfolded her in a loose embrace. "I don't trust myself with you," he said. He rested his cheek against hers. "I want to kiss you, touch you, make love to you." He pressed her cheek harder, rocked her from side to side. "And never ever stop."

Amy was silent, wondering if she was hearing him correctly.

"I didn't know, Amy," he continued. He drew back his head to gaze at her. "I swear I never knew I could feel this way. The burning need never goes away. It makes me crazy."

"I know."

"You too?"

She nodded. "Sometimes I think I can't stand it another day—but I do."

He laughed—a harsh, bitter sound. "Once, I even called here late at night just to hear your voice on the answering machine."

He kissed her, touched her hair, her eyes, her mouth like a blind man memorizing a face. His hands moved restlessly over her back and she sensed his growing urgency, but didn't have the will to stop him.

Suddenly, he stumbled to his feet, upsetting the chair in his haste. "I have to get out of here. Catch a plane. Go back to where I belong." He looked at her with desperation in his eyes, hesitated, then rushed out of the room.

Amy hurried after him, saw him grab his coat and head for the front door. He couldn't leave yet, she thought. She hadn't even had a chance to say goodbye. "Nathan, wait . . ."

He turned to face her. "Do you have the medicine pouch I gave you?" he asked. When she nodded, he added, "Promise me you will wear it."

She lifted her forlorn gaze to meet his. "I promise."

His dark eyes bored into hers. "Every day, Amy. There is danger in that town, and I cannot be here to protect you."

8

Amy hadn't slept the night before, and as she drove to Wheeler, her mind and body felt weighted down with hopelessness. Last fall when she and Nathan had parted, he'd said the thought of being away from her created an ache so terrible he didn't know if he could live with it. He was wrong. You went on living and the pain got worse—much worse.

Gunmetal gray clouds that matched her mood hovered just above the Douglas firs. The station wagon's windshield wipers labored to control the sheeting rain. She let out a long sigh. A little sunshine might have made the day bearable.

Once at the courthouse, she got soaked while dashing from the parking lot to the building's entry portico. Pushing open one of the double oak doors, she bumped into a man with wavy red hair who stepped back a few feet and peered at her through rimless glasses. "Uh . . . excuse me, you aren't Dr. Prescott"—he shook his head doubtfully—"Are you?"

Amy wiped the rain from her lashes and squinted up at him. His voice sounded vaguely familiar. "Yes. I mean, are you looking for me or my father?"

"You." He gestured toward a door off to the right. "The sheriff said you were on your way." He smiled and laugh lines fanned out from his blue eyes. "You're not exactly what I expected . . . I mean, people who do what you do don't usually look . . ." He turned pink and stuck out his hand. "I'm Jed MacManus, Dr. Nguyen's attorney."

She shook his hand and said, "We need to talk."

"Yes, we do. I'm late for court now. But . . ." His flush deepened. "Could we, uh . . . meet at the Cove in Ursa Bay at seven, possibly, and talk over dinner?" He gazed at her with an anxious expression.

She regarded him with a puzzled frown. The two times she'd talked to him on the phone, he'd sounded confident and able, yet here he was stammering like a schoolboy.

"Would that be all right?" he said after she didn't respond immediately. "I—I have to be in the area and . . . since we're going to be working as a team, we really should get acquainted. Don't you think?"

"Seven?" She calculated her day's schedule. "I might be able to make it. If not, perhaps my father can."

"Your father?" He seemed disappointed. "Oh yes, of course, you practice together, I'd forgotten."

"He knows as much about this case as I do," she said. "In any case, Mr. MacManus, you'll have to excuse me. I'm late. She brushed by him and headed for the sheriff's office.

Deputy Pierce, wearing a sullen expression, showed her to the jail's visiting room where Cam was seated and departed without a word.

Amy glanced at his retreating back and sat down across from Cam. "What's ailing the deputy?"

"Jed chewed him out for mouthing off."

Amy's opinion of the attorney rose a few points. "Is MacManus a friend of yours?"

"Met him a year ago when his mother was brought into the trauma center. So, tell me, have you learned anything?"

She drew a breath. It would be best to get the questions out of the way first. She pressed her palm against her stomach, which had begun to act up again. "Do you lift weights?"

Cam raised an eyebrow. "Occasionally. Why?"

"We found magnesium carbonate in the kitchen and bedroom."

He rubbed his forehead. "Antacids? Neither Mai nor I take them."

"Weight lifters sometimes use magnesium carbonate on their hands." She avoided his gaze. "Where do you go to work out?"

"Fenwick's, at the foot of Main. I play handball there twice a week. Well, I used to."

Amy jotted his answer in her notebook, then looked up at him. "What part of Cambodia did Mai come from?"

"She and Chantou seldom mentioned Cambodia. Once Mai said she thought her mother grew up in Phnom Penh."

"Are you interested in archaeology?"

He regarded her questioningly for a moment, then understanding lit his eyes. "The books in the study belong to Chantou. Mai said the subject fascinated him."

"I spoke with him at your wedding. He struck me as being an educated man. What do you know about him?"

"Less than nothing." Cam raised his shoulders in a shrug. "He read a lot. Kept up on what was going on in

Southeast Asia." He folded his arms. "What has Chantou got to do with Mai's murder?"

"Perhaps nothing." Amy lay her notebook on the counter. "Mai was right to be paranoid, Cam. Someone *was* spying on her."

"Oh, God"—Cam covered his face—"Why didn't I believe her?"

As gently as she could, Amy told him about the destructive search of the house, the evidence they'd found, and, when she could put it off no longer, the results of the autopsy.

When she finished, Cam sat as if stunned. "The man's a monster." His lip quivered. "He must be. Who else would do such a thing?"

Amy studied his face. "We think Mai knew him. Either that, or he had a key to the house."

"Mai had the locks changed two weeks ago. He couldn't have had a key, unless"—his eyes clouded—"she gave it to him" He gripped the edge of the counter.

Amy stretched out her hand in an effort to reach him. "We have to consider every possibility." She pushed a sheet of paper across to him. "We'll need a list of your male friends and acquaintances."

He recoiled. "You think someone I *know* did that to her?"

"Cam," she said gently. "Every day, you see what terrible things people are capable of doing."

"Not my friends. Not people I know."

Amy got to her feet. "How well do we really know anyone?" she asked.

From the outside, Fenwick's Athletic Club looked like many other red brick warehouses built in the early nineteen hundreds. Inside, in the U-shaped foyer, clear Plexiglas extended from floor to ceiling, providing a view of each room. On Amy's left, two men played handball; on her right, a group of women exercised to music.

She had stood watching the scene only a few minutes when a young blond woman came toward her. She wore royal blue slacks and a matching blouse trimmed with a white collar and cuffs. She was so thin, she looked anorexic. "May I help you?"

"I'm Amy Prescott," Amy said, noting the FAC logo rendered in script on the woman's collar. A blue plastic tag disclosed that her name was Daphne. "Do you offer low-impact aerobics for expectant mothers?"

"But definitely." The woman flashed a cover-girl smile. "It's an ongoing class and they're just starting today's workout. You can sit in, if you'd like."

Wondering if her stomach were up to the challenge, Amy forced a smile. "Yes, I'd like that."

Daphne took her name, then led her down the hall to a room where a group of women in various stages of pregnancy were sitting on blue vinyl mats. Amy took a seat on a vacant mat beside an Asian woman.

"Hi." Good humor glinted in the woman's dark eyes and wreathed her angular face. "I'm Hue Quoy."

Amy answered her smile. "Amy Prescott." The instructor began to speak, cutting off any further conversation.

When the session ended, Amy followed Hue down a flight of stairs to the windowless basement. As they started along a hallway, an Asian man with permed hair worn in an elaborate pompadour came toward them. He was dressed in the club's blue and white uniform and carried a stack of towels. He stopped near the group of women and a smile spread over his delicately formed features.

"Good morning, ladies. Are all the mothers in fine health today?"

A chorus of answers came from all sides. Hue grinned and a tiny dimple flickered beside her wide mouth. "They go bonkers when Kim's around." She rolled her eyes. "They think he's *soo* romantic looking."

They entered the women's dressing room. Dark blue walls absorbed light from the single overhead fixture and created a cave-like effect.

"Give me a few minutes to change and we'll walk out together," Hue said, scuttling down one of the rows of gray lockers that partitioned the room into long shadowy alleyways.

Amy strolled past the lockers en route to the lavatories. She stopped beside a woman who was changing her shoes and pointed to the combination locks attached to protruding hasps. "Are these dependable?"

"Usually," the woman said and giggled. "But they're stiff and I don't always get those long steel prongs pushed in far enough." She shrugged and turned her palms up. "Then they don't catch."

"I'll have to remember that." Amy pushed open the door to the lavatory. While she sponged her face with a wet paper towel, she thought over what the woman had said. If someone checked Cam's lock every time he came to play handball, they could have gotten lucky one day and found that the lock hadn't caught. Or there might be some way the lock could be altered so the steel prongs didn't fit into the cylinder properly. She jotted down a reminder to check with a locksmith and hurried out to meet Hue.

"You going to sign up?" the woman asked as they headed for the parking lot.

"I may. I live in Ursa Bay, but I might have to be in Wheeler quite often during the next few weeks."

"Oh, are you visiting someone?"

"No, I'm a private investigator." Amy opened her I.D. wallet and handed it to Hue.

Hue squinted her eyes as she read. "You're a doctor too?"

"That's right." Amy opened the passenger door of the station wagon. "Get in out of this drizzle and I'll explain." She shut the passenger door after Hue sat down, then went around to the driver's side, sliding behind the wheel.

Hue was looking at her with expectant admiration. "So, how did you come to be both a doctor *and* and a spy?"

Amy laughed. "My father was the medical examiner for Lomitas Island in the San Juans. Sometimes, in that capacity, he was able to solve crimes."

"Hey, just like on TV."

"Kind of." She grinned at Hue. "His work fascinated me. So, while most teenage girls were going out with boys, me and my father were going over a crime scene or examining a dead body."

Hue shivered and made a face. "You've *got* to be kidding."

"I've always been a little weird," Amy said with a laugh. "Anyway, to make a long story short, I got a degree in medicine, pathology, and forensic science. Then Dad and I set up our own forensic investigation business in Ursa Bay."

Hue frowned. "I still don't quite understand what you do."

"We try to determine cause in cases of questioned death." She angled her body so her brown eyes held the other woman's. "Hue, I'm a friend of Cam Nguyen's. I'm trying to find out who killed his wife, Mai."

Hue drew a quick, harsh breath and tears filmed her eyes.

Amy rested her hand on Hue's sleeve. "So you knew her?"

Hue bobbed her head. "We went through school together." She sighed and shook her head sadly. "Mai was so pretty, so full of life. And now she's gone."

"I know. I keep remembering how happy she looked at her wedding." Amy opened her notebook. "Cam says Mai changed after her father died. Did you see her after she moved back to Wheeler?"

"Only once." Hue bit her lip. "She *did* act strange."

"In what way?"

"Jumpy. We went to lunch. She kept looking over her shoulder as if . . ." Hue pulled a tissue from her purse and wiped her eyes. "As if she were afraid."

"Did you know her father?"

"Everyone did." She gestured toward the town. "He helped all of the families." She began to tear her tissue into shreds.

Amy played a hunch. "It's a shame they still haven't found the driver who ran him down. People like that should be punished."

Hue crushed the shredded tissue into a ball. "One of our people saw it happen."

Amy's eyes narrowed. "Did the person tell the authorities what he'd seen?"

"Oh, no, he won't tell anyone." Hue twisted her fingers together, swallowed, and stole a look at Amy. "He's terrified. He thinks he'll be killed, too."

9

Dread chilled Amy as she pulled up into the Nguyens' driveway. She chewed half a dozen soda crackers and drank some clear soup from a thermos, trying to vanquish the familiar wave of nausea. Finally, there was no other excuse for not going into the house.

She checked the .38 in her shoulder holster. As she withdrew her hand, it brushed against the white doeskin medicine pouch that hung between her breasts. The previous fall, when Nathan feared she might die, he had placed it around her neck. He'd said the articles within would protect her—and they had. Now its spiritual powers had to protect not only her but the lives she carried inside her as well.

With a tired sigh, she turned up her collar to shield her from the raw wind that was blowing and carried her equipment to the back porch. Stalling a moment longer, she studied Pran's greenhouses. Had the perpetrator worked there, perhaps? Was that how he had managed to come and go as he pleased?

Her attention shifted to the wind-tossed fir grove where they now knew Mai's attacker had waited. In among the thrashing branches, she thought she saw something black and solid.

She shivered, lugged her gear into the ransacked kitchen, locked the door, and propped a chair against it.

Her first full breath filled her nostrils with the odor of incense. Her heart slammed against her ribs. *He's here.*

She took out her gun, braced her arms in front of her, and eased into the living room. On the floor by the glass patio doors, a six-foot feather palm sprawled atop strewn black soil. A lacy Ming Aralia and a green-veined white caladium hung limp from empty porcelain pots.

She shivered. The killer hadn't yet found what he wanted. She moved from room to room, opening drapes, throwing wide closet doors, and checking behind furniture.

At last satisfied she was alone in the house, she changed into jeans, donned gloves and knee pads, and began an inspection of the polished wood floors. Mai's barefooted killer had to have left a sole print.

An hour's search turned up several clear prints in the living room. She set a camcorder on a tripod to pan the area, then positioned an overturned coffee can containing a sixty-watt bulb near the print, inverted a small fish tank over that, and set a fingerprint camera down on the floor within arm's reach.

When ready, she soaked a cotton ball in sodium hydroxide solution, lay it in a small ceramic dish, added Super Glue, lifted the fish tank, and set the dish on the hot coffee can.

Gradually, the heat and fuming agent worked its magic and a whitish-colored sole print appeared. She snapped pictures and moved the entire setup to the next section of flooring.

At some point in her routine, Amy got the distinct feeling that someone was watching her. Without lifting her head, she checked the patio doors. Nothing. Rising, she pretended to reach for her forensic satchel but instead grabbed the camcorder handle and swung it toward the front windows.

Fear ballooned in her chest.

A man in a black hood was crouched in the shrubbery, his lips drawn back in a animal-like snarl. His dark eyes glinted menacingly through the slitted cloth. Cold. Evil. Deadly. Then he vanished.

10

Amy checked her coat and lined up behind several other people in the restaurant's foyer. She straightened the navy blue jacket of her maternity outfit. The one that had made her feel so good the day she'd met Nathan. Now, it appeared to bulge in all the wrong places.

Her shoulders drooped. Not even twenty-four hours had elapsed since Nathan left and already the loneliness had returned twofold.

She tried to take some interest in her surroundings but didn't succeed. Seashell pink walls and aquamarine carpeting set off brass ships' sextants, portholes, and bells. Weariness weighed down her eyes and she could feel the beginning of a headache. If she'd had any sense, she'd have stayed home.

When the maître d' spoke her name, she knew it was too late to back out. She was escorted to a window table with a view of the San Juan Islands in the distance.

As she approached, Jed MacManus got to his feet and beamed at her. He pulled out her chair. "I'm glad you could make it."

As she smiled at him, an image of the hooded man at the Nguyen house flashed into her mind. She'd taken a long, roundabout route home to assure she wasn't followed. "I wasn't certain I would for awhile there."

He seated himself across from her. "Oh no?"

"I'll tell you about it after you read this." She handed him an envelope containing her father's autopsy report and a transcript of their current investigative report.

He read swiftly, underlining items as he scanned each page. When he finished, he tucked the envelope in the pocket of his brown tweed blazer and sighed. "Not too helpful, I'm afraid. The prosecutor will contend that Cam tortured and raped his wife."

"Unless the DNA on the semen proves otherwise."

"He could still accuse Cam of hiring the killer." Jed stowed his rimless glasses in a case in the pocket of his green shirt. "Speaking of the killer, do you have any idea why the man keeps coming back to ransack the house? Why would he take the risk of getting caught?"

"Whatever he's looking for must mean a lot to him." Amy took a sip of ice water. "He returned to the house again today."

Jed's features sharpened. "How do you know?"

Before she could reply, the waiter appeared. When they had ordered, Amy took another sip of water. "I think he left the house a few minutes before I arrived."

Jed sat forward. "Was the sheriff with you?"

"No—"

"Good God, you didn't go there alone, did you?"

She stared back at him, her jaw set. "I did, yes. It's my job."

"That may be, Dr. Prescott, but you won't be of much use to Cam or anyone else if your foolishness gets you killed."

Amy folded her arms. "I've managed to look after myself just fine up to now."

Jed's nostrils flared. "That's not the point. He could have shown up while you were there."

"He did!" She realized her voice sounded shrill. *Relax. Take deep breaths.* Why was she getting so upset? she wondered.

"Jesus Christ, are you crazy?" he said.

Her throat closed up. *Not now.* She squeezed her hands together. Tears gathered at the corners of her eyes. *Shit!* She hated the weakness she felt, her bone tiredness. She hated him for speaking to her in such a way. If any man was going to chew her out, it should be Nathan. She blinked back her tears. *Damn men. Damn a world where nothing came out right.*

"Hey, I'm sorry." Jed viewed her with an anxious expression. "You've had quite a scare and I'm not helping matters." He peered at her with concern in his eyes. "You okay?"

She nodded as a tear escaped her eye; she wiped it away with her fingers. "I don't know what's wrong with me." She bit her lip and smiled tremulously. "I'm sorry."

"Look, I understand, Amy." He cocked his head. "Do you mind if I call you Amy? For months, Cam's been telling me what a terrific person you are. I feel like I know you."

"Terrific person?" Another tear escaped her eyes. "Terrible mess is more like it."

Jed's beeper went off then, and much to her relief the attorney went off to find a phone. By the time he returned, she had managed to get her emotions under control.

She forced a feeble smile. "I don't know what came over me. I'm usually not such a wimp."

"Hey, don't give it another thought. You're looking at one of the afflicted. A bleeding divorce casualty."

Amy grimaced. "I've been there."

He grinned and his blue eyes lit up. "What's a nice lady like you doing in this mean business anyway?"

She settled back in her chair. "I guess my father's to blame." She told him how she'd gotten involved in forensics at a rather young age. "I've never considered doing anything else." She gave him a sheepish glance. "Today, my personal life kind of caved in on me."

He nodded. "Once that happened to me while I was doing my summation for the jury." He made a face. "I don't know who was more embarrassed by my tears—them or me."

She squared her shoulders. "About this afternoon. The man I saw was wearing a knit hood over his head. I didn't see his face."

"Where did you see him?"

"He was watching me from outside." Amy shuddered. "I've never seen such hate-filled eyes," she said as the waiter set down the seafood dish she'd ordered. She hoped the meal would be gentle to her stomach.

Jed sliced off a piece of his fillet mignon and chewed thoughtfully. "You have any theories about what the guy is after?"

"Did Cam tell you Mai's father was killed by a hit-and-run driver?" Amy tasted the dish and found it to be delicious.

Jed frowned. "No. I mean, I knew her father was dead, but that's all."

"Dad and I think the two deaths might be connected."

"Really?" He mixed sour cream, butter, and bacon bits into his potato and sampled the results with a satisfied expression. "I got the contents of Pran's safety deposit box today."

Amy leaned forward. "Find anything interesting?"

"Haven't looked yet." He brushed a piece of parsley to the edge of his plate. "Cam refuses to believe his wife was interested in another man. He hoped Pran's personal effects might give him a clue as to Mai's emotional state the last few months of her life." Jed sliced off anther piece of steak. "So, why'd you go back to the Nguyen house?"

"To look for sole prints. The ones I took today show that our suspect has a triangular scar on his right heel and that he's flatfooted."

"Won't do you much good unless the man is caught."

"We may be getting closer. I lifted a fingerprint from underneath the toilet lid."

Jed grinned. "Smart lady." He regarded her with a steady gaze. "Amy, may I see you again?"

Amy set down her fork. "I don't think that's a good idea. My life is a shambles right now."

"Mine too. Any other reasons?"

She shifted uneasily in her seat before deciding the best way to discourage him would be to tell the truth. "Actually, I'm in love with someone. He recently married someone else."

"Maybe I could help you forget him."

She smiled. "That wouldn't be too easy, Jed. In about five months, I'm going to have a couple of very lively reminders."

For an instant, he looked startled. Then he let out a hearty laugh. "Cam sure described you well. A certain Prescott panache, that's what he calls it."

Amy laughed with him.

"I'd still like to see you," Jed said.

"You've got to be kidding. Before long, I'll be big as a blimp."

"Look, I'm thirty-five years old and right now I don't want to even *think* about getting married again." He ran his hand over his face. "Amy, what I really need is a friend."

She felt a tightness in her chest. "So do I."

"Great. How about sharing a piece of chocolate truffle cheese cake with me?"

She groaned. "I'll probably regret it, but I'm game."

After dinner, they sat in his Porsche while Jed went through the contents of Mai's father's safe deposit box. "Most of this seems to pertain to Mr. Pran's property and business."

Jed stacked a number of legal documents on the seat beside him. "Hmm, what do we have here?" The long white envelope had a glob of red sealing wax on its flap. "He instructed that this not to be opened until his death." Jed examined the unbroken seal. "I wonder why Mai didn't look at it?"

"Perhaps she knew the contents."

"How could she?"

"Her father lived several hours after the hit-and-run driver struck him. Mai was with him most of the time."

"Maybe you and your father are right. The two deaths might be related." He slit open the top of the envelope with a pen knife, pulled out a sheet of paper, and scanned it quickly. "Listen to this," he said. "It's a letter from Mr. Pran to Mai. 'Most precious daughter, What is revealed here you must tell to no one—not your husband, nor your dearest friend. The Khmer Rouge's demons of death have found their way to our small village. It is my fervent hope that a day will come when Kampuchea will be free of the nightmare the Khmer Rouge has created and Buddha can once again look upon beauty. Then I beseech you to remember your favorite childhood game and restore the Enlightened One's sight. One last word, dear child, and I caution you again never to repeat this. After we came to America, our sponsor died. To insure our safety, I assumed his identity. My birth name is Taun Keo.' "

11

Amy crossed the bridge spanning the Wasku River on the way to her morning aerobics class. Muddy water churned over the banks and surged over a tree that had fallen into the raging torrent. If the rain didn't stop soon, the valley would be flooded.

Amy refused to let that gloomy thought dampen her high spirits. Today, for a number of reasons, the whole world had a rosy cast. She had woken up without feeling nauseous for the first time in weeks, and Hue had informed her that she may have persuaded the person who witnessed the hit-and-run of Mai's father to talk to her.

Humming a tune, she parked in the athletic club's lot and dashed inside. She smiled at Hue as she plopped down on her mat. "How'd you make out?" she asked.

"We can go there after class."

"That's wonderful."

"He has conditions," Mai added, but when the instructor of the class launched into the first exercise she whispered, "I'll tell you later."

Although the routine wasn't rigorous, Amy knew she had muscles by the time the session ended. She gave a small groan as she got into Hue's compact car. "What kind of conditions?" She asked, picking up where they had left off.

"Many of our people lived in Cambodia during Pol Pot's reign of terror. Ghosts of the Khmer Rouge's harvest of death still haunt them. This man yearns to live out his life in peace."

"Will he talk to me?"

Hue drove out of the lot and headed toward the main part of town. "Yes." She glanced at Amy and quickly away. "But refuses to give you his name or to let you see his face." She sighed. "You do understand, don't you?"

"Absolutely. I'll be grateful for whatever information he can give me."

"Good." Hue traveled two blocks before she continued. "I arranged for him to meet us at a friend's restaurant. He'll be on one side of a screen, you and I will be on the other. I'll interpret." She turned up an alley and halted behind a two-story wooden building that housed the Angkor Temple Restaurant.

Amy touched her arm. "Thank you for your help, Hue."

Hue met her gaze. "It's nowhere near enough. Mai was a good friend." She stepped out onto the shale-covered roadway and looked around quickly before beckoning to Amy. "We'll go in the back door. It'll be best if we aren't seen."

Inside, Hue led her down a corridor to a room with a wall-sized painting of the temples of Angkor Wat. On other walls, images of richly adored celestial maidens, their arms and fingers curved gracefully, danced and sang for Khmer royalty.

At one end of the room, Amy observed a white silk

four-panel screen blocking off a corner. Hue took one of the low stools beside a short-legged table, motioned Amy to the other, and poured tea into thin chinaware cups. "Now, what do you need to know?" she asked.

"Anything he can tell me about the car."

Hue took a sip of tea, then started to speak in Khmer to the man behind the screen.

The man replied in a thin, quavery voice. Hue turned to Amy. "A Japanese model. Fairly new. Blue like spring sky."

"Did he see the license?"

"Only an A and a four."

"That's better than nothing. Did he know the driver?"

After Hue had asked the question, the man was silent. Hue frowned and shook her head.

Finally, Amy heard the man answer in a whisper. Hue said, "He didn't know him then, but he's seen him since." Hue stared down at the table for several minutes. "He is one of the *yavana*. If the shopkeepers don't pay them, their shops are burned."

Hue's remark didn't surprise Amy. Nathan had sensed the people's fear. Although she guessed what the answer would be to her next question, she felt she had to try. "Will he identify the man if he's arrested?"

To Amy's astonishment the man responded to her directly with a hissed "No." Then he reverted to his own language.

When he stopped speaking, Hue stood up. "That's all he'll say."

They left the restaurant then, and Hue drove Amy back to her station wagon in Fenwick's lot. Amy thanked Hue again, then remembered the mysterious woman with whom Cam said he'd spent the evening the night Mai died. "Hue, do you know a Chea Le?"

Hue shook her head. "She's not from around here." She waved and drove away.

Amy stopped off at the courthouse to pick up the list Cam had made her of his friends, then headed for home. As she cruised along the two-lane road, she ticked off items on a mental list. The caretakers of the greenhouse had been eliminated. Cam said the three men were elderly and had worked for Pran for years. Tomorrow, she'd have to start questioning Cam's acquaintances.

She topped the hill and started into the switchbacks. As she came out of the first curve, she braked to slow her speed. The pedal smacked on the floorboards.

No brakes. She pumped the pedal. *Nothing. Shift down. Shift down.* Metal ground against spinning metal, refusing to mesh. Adrenaline racing her pulse, she steered toward the pavement's edge, hoping the gravel shoulder would slow the car. Crushed rock caught her tire, jerked her to the right, sent her skidding toward jagged basalt slabs.

Amy spun the wheel frantically and the vehicle straightened, picked up speed, and veered into the outside lane. On the incline below, she glimpsed a logging truck.

Cold sweat broke out along her spine. Blasting the horn, she yanked the steering wheel, swinging the station wagon back to the inside lane. It pulled sideways. One fender grating a rock shelf, she careened around a corner and angled into a sweeping S-turn. *Too fast.*

Tires squealing, the car jounced off a guardrail and corrected its course. She grabbed the hand brake. Acrid fumes billowed through the air vents.

Fir saplings growing at the road's edge slapped the windows as she raced by. The speeding automobile created its own deep-throated roar. She fed in the clutch again. Metal screeched in protest. The station wagon fishtailed and spun in a wide arc toward the ravine.

Please, Lord, I can't die now. The car caromed off a boulder, whipping her head back, then veered back toward the cliff face. Brown water cascaded down from the bluff above, carrying bushes, rocks, and debris. She swerved and the fender raked a screeching scar.

Ahead, the logging truck rounded the curve, its massive load of cedar logs swinging into her lane.

No room. Can't make it. Nathan, help me, help me.

The station wagon ripped a path through the dense vegetation. Limbs snapped and thudded against the floorboards. Thundering on, the machine plunged up and over a talus ridge and for a horrifying moment became airborne. Amy gripped the wheel and prayed.

The vehicle landed with a grating, shuddering, teeth-jarring crash. Her head snapped forward, hit something hard.

Darkness.

12

"Lady. Hey, lady."

Amy felt a cold wet cloth on her face. Someone shook her shoulder. When she opened her eyes, pain ricocheted inside her head. "What happened?"

"You damn near scared the shit outa me, that's what happened." The man's sandy hair bristled from his scalp like an angry porcupine. "Never saw such crazy drivin'. You trying to kill yourself or somethin'?"

"Brakes failed," she said in a whisper; talking any louder caused rockets to go off in her throbbing skull. She took the sodden red bandanna from him and pressed it against her forehead.

"No shit!" The man grinned. "Lady, you sure as hell got balls. I get nightmares about my rig goin' wild. Them friggin' logs would squash me flatter'n a piss ant at a picnic." He peered at her. "You want to ride into Wheeler with me?"

"No"—she motioned to her cellular phone—"I'll call a tow truck in Ursa Bay." She switched the wet bandanna to her left hand, retrieved her purse from the floor, and took out her notebook. "What's your name?"

"Doug Hawley. I work for Cascade Logging. You sure you shouldn't see a doctor?"

She cleared her throat and managed to speak in a stronger voice. "I *am* a doctor."

"Okay, I hope you know what you're doin'." He closed her car door.

She rolled down the window to hand him his bandanna. "Thanks for helping out."

"Keep it. You need it worse than I do." He started off, then slogged back through the wet salal, bracken fern, and huckleberry bushes. "I'll tell the sheriff you're here."

She made a face. "I'd rather not see him, but I guess I'll have to."

Smile lines spread across his craggy features. "Yeah, he's a real double-domed fathead, ain't he? If he knew half as much as he thinks he does, he could graduate from the third grade. You take care now."

She stretched her legs and moaned. She ached all over, her fingers, her knees, her legs, her feet. She closed her eyes, tried to form a plan.

Her father would have to know. She gathered her strength and called him first. "I've had an accident," she said, trying to keep her voice steady.

"Are you all right?"

"A few bumps is all." She began to shiver and had to concentrate on every word. "I'm going to have Northwest Auto Repair give me a tow."

"You want me to come get you?"

She braced her quaking body against the door frame. "That's not necessary. I'm waiting for Sheriff Boyce."

"You sound funny. Are you sure you're okay?"

"I th-think so-so, Dad," she stammered.

"Like hell. Where are you?"

"W-West side of the first hill out of Wheeler," she replied.

"You got a blanket?"

"Yes."

"Wrap it around you and prop your feet up. I'll be there as soon as I can."

By evening, she had seen a doctor and her car had been examined. Miraculously, both of them had come through the ordeal with only minor scrapes and bruises. She still felt a trifle rocky, but didn't know whether that was due to the accident or to the fact that she had decided to call Nathan.

She picked up the receiver twice before she overcame her nervousness enough to punch in his number.

When he answered, in the background, she heard a Patsy Cline ballad. Her flesh began to quiver. "Nathan, this is Amy."

"Amy! She heard a thud, a thump, and then the song ended abruptly.

She heard him take a deep breath. Without being in his room, she knew where his mind had been, how his body had reacted to the sound of her voice. In the one night they'd spent together, she'd learned the depth of his passion.

"Amy, what is it, what's wrong?" His tone was steady, calm.

She tried to mimic it. "I need to ask you something, Nathan. "Did you see all of the five employees who work at the athletic club in Wheeler?"

He hesitated for a moment. "No. One of the Asians works the evening shift. What's wrong?"

"I was there today. I parked my car at Fenwick's and later at the courthouse. On my way home, my brakes failed. The garage says the brake line was punctured."

"Were you hurt?"

She forced a laugh. "Only a bruised knee and a big knot on my forehead."

He let out his breath. "Thank God. I knew something had happened to you."

"What do you mean?" she asked.

"I sensed you were in danger. I thought I heard you call my name."

"I might have. It was a very close call."

He groaned. "Amy, you've seen what this person is capable of. Let someone else take over the investigation."

"I can't do that, Nathan."

"Then don't go *anywhere* alone."

"I'm nearly finished in Wheeler. I've learned a few things about the hit-and-run. And that Mai's father's name is Taun Keo, not Chantou Pran."

"How did you find that out?"

"Jed found a letter in Pran's safety deposit box."

There was a measured silence before he responded. "Jed?"

"Sorry," Amy said. "Jed MacManus—Cam's lawyer."

"How much do you know about him?"

She frowned, puzzled. "I met him last night for the first time. Why? Do you know something I don't?"

Another silence. "He's there. I'm here."

Her heart gave a wrench. "I'm not looking for a man to replace you, Nathan."

"I'm sorry . . ." He swallowed. "Amy, when I was with you, I got the impression you weren't quite well. Is everything all right?"

Amy steadied herself. "Just a little stomach upset. Stress, probably. I'm fine, really."

"It's been four months since we made love. If there was something I should know about, you would tell me, wouldn't you?"

Her pulse quickened. "Of course, Nathan," she said.

13

B.J. took up the task of interviewing Cam's friends while Amy recuperated at the office, keeping an ice pack on her swollen knee. She winced at the bruises on her face every time she looked in the mirror, and thanked God she had gotten through the accident relatively unscathed. She used the time to get her lab and paperwork up to date.

Four days later, she drove to Harborview Medical Center in Seattle to speak to the supervisor of the hospital's volunteers.

When Amy walked into the office, she approached a woman seated behind an oak desk, who peered at her over half glasses. "How may I help you?" the woman asked.

Amy handed her one of her business cards. "I'm investigating the murder of Dr. Nguyen's wife."

"Terrible. Absolutely terrible." The woman removed her glasses and tucked a tendril of graying hair into place. "How do you do? I'm Nancy Waring. I simply cannot believe that nice doctor would ever do such an awful thing."

"That's why I'm here, Mrs. Waring. Cam says he had

dinner that night with Chea Le, one of your volunteers. Would it be possible for me to talk to her?"

"Chea Le? Let me check." She repositioned her glasses, leafed through a file, and drew out a card. "Looks as if she hasn't reported in for over a week."

"Do you have a number where she can be reached?"

"There's only a reference number and a phone where messages can be left."

"Could I have those and her address?"

"I'm not sure whether . . ." She stood up and smoothed her navy blue skirt over plump hips. "Excuse me just one moment." She took Amy's business card and left the room.

Ten minutes later, Mrs. Waring bustled back into the room. "My goodness, I had no idea you were related to Dr. B.J. Prescott."

Amy smiled. "He's my father."

"I'm always reading about him in the papers." Her cheeks turned pink. "Such a fine, intelligent man. And so distinguished looking." She wrote down some information on a sheet of paper and handed it to Amy. "You must be very proud of him."

Amy thanked her and hurried out to use her car phone. When she found that both the numbers the woman had given her were no longer in service, she consulted her city map and set out to find the address Mrs. Waring had provided. It turned out to be a vacant building.

After consulting her notes, she drove to the upscale apartment complex where Cam had said he'd gone after he and Chea Le had dinner.

She knocked on the manager's door. A man with a slim, aesthetic face opened the door. He wore a pewter gray suit of Italian silk, a platinum gray shirt, and a contrasting tie. "Mr. Pham?" she asked, addressing him by the name engraved on the door.

He studied her with an arrogant expression, unclamped his lips, and said, "Yes?"

"I'm Dr. Amy Prescott." She showed him her I.D.

"Investigator?" He eyed her narrowly. "Why are you here?"

"I need to ask you a few questions." She eased her foot past the doorjamb. "Could I come in?"

"I see people only by appointment."

"I'll only take a few minutes." He moved back just far enough for her to plant both feet in the deep white pile of the foyer carpet. She opened her notebook. "On January tenth of this year, did a Miss Chea Le occupy apartment 105?"

A muscle tensed in his cheek and he took a quick, shallow breath. "No one lives in apartment 105. It is the one I show prospective residents."

Amy took her time recording his statement. When she glanced up, she saw the man swallow nervously. She fastened her steady gaze on him. "Did Chea Le bring a man to that apartment on the evening of January tenth?"

"I do not have a tenant by that name."

"Mr. Pham, did a man and a woman occupy 105 for several hours that evening?"

His features froze into a tense mask. "No."

Amy closed her notebook. "May I see the apartment?"

He folded his arms and glared at her. "I'm afraid that is impossible."

"I can easily get a search warrant, sir." She issued up a silent prayer.

Tight ridges formed on either side of Mr. Pham's

mouth. "I'll give you exactly ten minutes and no more. I have people coming."

"That will be sufficient." She held out her hand. "May I have the key?"

"No, you may not," he said. He retrieved a ring of keys from his desk, then motioned for her to follow him. It was only a short way down the hall to number 105. The chances were highly unlikely that anyone could have used the apartment without his knowledge, Amy determined.

He flung open the door and stood back for her to enter. A sweep of sand-colored carpeting issued into a living room with champagne walls and furniture in muted shades of green and marsh brown. She observed the nubby-textured wool upholstery and continued on into the bedroom, where jade green damask hung from brass drapery rods and also covered a king-sized bed.

Mr. Pham followed at her heels until suddenly his phone shrilled from down the hall. He flung an agitated glance in her direction, excused himself, and left the room.

Amy hurried into the living room, took a pair of scissors from her purse, and snipped fibers from the back of each piece of furniture. She was able to bag the fibers before Mr. Pham returned. She met him at the door with a nonchalant smile. "I believe I've seen all I need to see," she said. "Thank you for being so gracious."

On her way back to Ursa Bay to have lunch with Jed MacManus, she wondered what Mr. Pham's response would have been if she had mentioned the *yavana*, the Khmer Rouge, or the harvest of death.

* * *

Amy waited for Jed at Jack's Café and Bookstore. Knotty pine shelves stuffed with books bracketed her table on two sides. A third side gave a view of Ursa Bay's polished granite courthouse, the town's architectural monument to the wealthy founders of the town and their equally well-to-do descendants.

Jed arrived just as the big courthouse clock chimed the hour. "Why the cynical expression?" he asked, pulling out a chair.

"Just thinking about our affluent citizenry."

Jed laughed. "This is one town where you don't dare talk about anybody. I nearly blew my practice before I realized most of the people in Ursa Bay are interrelated." He picked up the menu. "You think a bowl of clam chowder will warm the inner man?"

"It ought to help." She ordered a bowl, too. When they were alone, she took a brown envelope and her notebook from her purse. "My father checked out Cam's male acquaintances. All but two have alibis."

"He'll keep on digging, won't he?"

"You can count on it. He ran all the fingerprints we've found through Seattle's automated I.D. system." She blew out her breath. "Our suspect—or suspects—has never been arrested. And the license numbers of Fenwick's employees didn't give us any leads either. The Caucasians don't have records and the two Asians apparently don't own cars."

"What did you find out about the woman Cam was with the night Mai was murdered."

Amy explained about Chea Le's sham address and the disconnected phones. "The apartment where Cam claims she took him is a demonstrator. The manager denies ever knowing Miss Le, or that anyone ever used the apartment."

"So where's that leave you?"

"I'll go over the clothes Cam wore and try to match them with the fibers I took from the apartment. Maybe I'll find something that will prove he was there."

"That's all the hope you can give me?"

"When Cam played handball at Fenwick's Athletic Club, he put his house keys in his locker. Combination locks can be fixed so they won't close properly."

"So somebody could have made copies of Cam's keys."

"Next time I see Cam, I'll find out where he keeps his gym bag."

"I've arranged Cam's bail. He needs to be out to make preparations for the Buddhist funeral."

Amy felt a sharp stab of remorse. "I've been so engrossed in this darned investigation, I'd forgotten about Mai."

Jed looked equally guilt-ridden. "I'm ashamed to say it, but that goes with the territory."

Amy sighed, opened her notebook, and ran her finger down the list she'd made. "We found a half-eaten piece of caramel candy in the woods where our suspect conducted a stakeout. The forensic dentist I sent it to says the man has a chipped front tooth."

"Oh, brother! Now we have a guy who smokes Djarum cigarettes, has flat feet, and a chipped tooth. So where the hell is he?"

Amy dumped the contents of a brown envelope on the table. "These are snapshots a friend of mine took of some of Wheeler's residents."

Jed put on his glasses, shuffled through the five-by-sevens, and handed them back. "Doesn't mean much to me."

She singled out a picture. "See this man, with the cap pulled down low?"

"Yes. What about him?"

She chose a photo from several she hadn't shown him. "This is an enlargement of his face."

"Good Lord, he's got a chipped front tooth. Who is he?"

"I don't know." She laid another photo on the table. "This is a blowup of the hooded man I saw last time I was at Cam's house."

"Ugh. No wonder he scared you."

"Notice his teeth?"

"I'll be damned." Jed's face lit up. "Hey, all we have to do is take these pictures and show them around Wheeler. Somebody is bound to identify him."

She shook her head. "Not if he's one of the *yavana* they fear."

Jed regarded her intently as a shaft of sunshine momentarily flooded through the window, crossing over her face. He leaned across the table. "Amy, what happened to you?"

She grimaced. "Are they still noticeable? My brakes failed a few days ago. I rapped my head on the windshield."

"Jesus, Amy, are you okay? And the babies?"

"We're all fine. A bit of a scare though. My car was tampered with."

"Are you sure?"

"Positive."

He regarded her with a grave expression. "I need solid evidence to get Cam off, but goddamn it, Amy, it's not worth your life."

14

Amy entered the prayer hall with Hue and found a secluded corner. She had never been to a Buddhist temple, and the unfamiliar setting made her nervous. She had expected to find a gathering of friends. Yet aside from the monks, she and Hue were the only mourners present.

"Look at all the gifts," Hue said, pointing to an alcove where gleaming multiple images of the Buddha were enshrined. On a dais below the images were wooden, china, and crockery bowls containing fruit and other articles of food. A pleased expression wreathed Hue's face. "Many people have been here."

The monk's soft musical chanting filled the temple, and within minutes, Amy found herself becoming relaxed and peaceful.

Hue gestured to the monks. "They chant to help Mai release positive energies."

Amy nodded in a rather dazed manner. A kaleidoscope of sights, smells, and sounds crowded her senses—incense, subdued lights, dozens of candle flames reflecting off the gleaming Buddha statues.

Hue went forward, laid the food she and Amy had

prepared on the alter in front of the Buddha, knelt, and prayed, then rejoined Amy.

"The state of a person's mind when he or she dies determines their rebirth," Hue said in a low voice. "People who die violently run a great risk."

Amy stared at her. "But that's not right. The way Mai died wasn't her fault."

"These days the priests take that into account. However, there was a time when the body of a woman who had gone through any violence, even childbirth, was not allowed in the temple."

Her statement rankled Amy but she kept her feelings about the sexist practice to herself. "When will Mai be cremated?"

"When the priests feel they've done as much as they can for her lingering spirit."

Amy watched as Cam shuffled into the temple flanked on either side by a priest in golden-colored robes. Tears stung her eyes. Cam's face was ashen, his eyes dull and lusterless.

Hue touched her arm and whispered, "He'll want to be alone."

Outside, Amy dried her eyes and blew her nose. "Justice! Mai never harmed anyone in her whole life. But she's dead and the man who killed her is out there and"—her voice broke and she swallowed to clear the lump in her throat—"and I still don't have the faintest idea who the rotten bastard is."

"You'll find him, Amy." Hue patted her arm. "I know you will."

The next morning, Amy sat at the conference table drizzling honey over a toasted English muffin while B.J.

watched her with an expression of disbelief. "This can't be my daughter. She's eating without me nagging her."

Amy laughed. "I had cereal, juice, and toast an hour ago, but I'm still hungry." She cocked her head and grinned at him. "And you're just jealous because you can't have honey on your muffin."

"Damn right, I am." The cordless phone at his elbow rang. He picked it up and answered, "Dr. B.J. Prescott here." He cradled the receiver between cheek and shoulder, pulled a scratch pad toward him, and picked up a pencil. "What's his name? He worked the evening shift? When did you find him?" He scribbled some notes. "How'd he die? The sheriff been notified? Good. Don't let anyone touch anything. We'll be there in about thirty minutes."

B.J. lay down the phone. "That was Cam. He stayed with friends in Seattle last night. Today, he went to Wheeler to make sure everything was all right at Pran's greenhouses. The day workers said when they arrived this morning, they found Gan Haing, the night man, dead."

"Homicide?"

"Nothing to indicate that. Could have been a heart attack. He was sixty years old."

"The sheriff coming?" When her father nodded, she stood up. "We'd better get going before he decides to take Cam into custody again."

By a stroke of good fortune, they drove into the parking area of the Nguyen house at the same time that Sheriff Boyce and Dr. Homer Epps, the coroner, pulled up. While B.J. greeted the men, Amy looked around her. Five of the gabled greenhouses had cement floors, glass walls, and adjustable glass panels in the roof. The other four consisted of wooden frameworks covered with clear plastic sheeting.

Cam, his small-boned features drawn into tense, haggard lines, beckoned from the middle glassed-in structure. Amy and the three men joined him. "He's down at the far end," Cam said. He led the way between rows of benches holding green plastic pots filled with red, pink, and lavender geraniums.

A spice fragrance scented the warm humid air, reminding Amy of summer gardens, but the sight of the still, white-haired man lying on a layer of burlap bags shattered the illusion.

B.J. halted the group some distance away. "Cam, how many people have been in here this morning?"

"Three. Me and two of the workers."

"Is that where they found him?"

Cam nodded. "He was lying on his face. They'd turned him on his back and laid him on the sacks just before I arrived."

Sheriff Boyce grunted. "A man can't die a natural death around here without everybody getting all excited."

B.J. swung around. "I'd rather protect the scene than regret it later." He squatted on his heels and studied the area of cement floor on which the man lay.

After noting an exit door beyond the body, Amy hurried back the way she'd come and circled around the outside. When she reached the rear of the building, she stopped. A fifteen-foot section of soil lay between the front greenhouse and the one behind it. The rain had let up around one that morning. Since then, it was evident that someone had crossed the area—someone wearing thongs.

She searched out the workmen and asked if any of them wore thongs. None did. She glanced from one man to the next and asked if any damage had been done to the greenhouse buildings.

"Many of the potted plants were uprooted," one man said, and pointed to one of the buildings.

She persuaded them to work elsewhere until she could film the damage and rushed back to the group. "He was here, Dad. He came in through the rear door."

The sheriff shot her an irritated glance. "Just how do you know that?"

"Our suspect wears thongs."

"So you say. What's to stop *my* suspect here"—he waved a hand at Cam, who eyed him with an angry expression—"from putting on a pair and tracking up the place to throw suspicion off of himself?"

B.J. rose to his feet. "Amy, go open the back door and take some pictures."

"Now just wait a damn minute, Prescott." Sheriff Boyce glowered at B.J. "I'm the one who's running this show."

B.J.'s face darkened. "The death of Mai Nguyen, her father, and this man are all related."

"You're off your nut." Boyce gave Cam a walleyed look. "Did you do in her old man too?"

Cam's steady gaze met and held the bigger man's. "I didn't kill anyone, Mr. Boyce."

"You don't fool me, New-Yen, or Win, or whatever the hell your name is. You're guilty as hell."

"Now, Fred." Dr. Homer Epps straightened his thin, sloping shoulders garbed in a brown, double-breasted suit and clasped his hands together in front of his chest. "The judge and the prosecuting attorney might not approve of—"

"Who the hell cares? This thing is getting out of hand."

"You're right, Sheriff," B.J. said in a controlled voice. "There's something rotten going on in Wheeler. You'd be wise to let us gather the proper evidence, otherwise your prosecuting attorney could end up with a damned red face. Most places that's a good way for a sheriff to get himself fired."

Boyce ran a hand over his face and shifted his feet. "Well, if you're gonna do something, do it. I ain't got all day."

Cam accompanied Amy to her father's van and helped carry her gear around back. "Are you going to stay in the house?" she asked him as she recorded the film number in the log she kept.

"I can't bring myself to even open the door," he answered.

"Perhaps Hue Quoy and I could straighten up the place and—"

"No. I'll call a housecleaning service." He let out a long sigh. "I'll never be able to live there. Maybe I can rent it." He made a vague gesture. "Shit, I can't think straight enough to make a decision right now."

She put her arm around his shoulders. "Things can wait. And if you need someone to talk to, you know my number."

He squeezed her hand. "Thanks, Amy, I don't know how I'll ever repay you and your father for what you're doing."

She patted his back and jerked her head toward the greenhouse. "I'd better get busy before the tension inside blows the roof off."

Being careful where she placed her feet, she opened the rear door and took the necessary pictures. "Okay, Dad, you can move him now. There's a footprint here I want to lift."

While her father and Dr. Epps examined the body, Amy marked off the area with crime tape and asked Cam to bring in one of the kits.

"What's this?" he asked, crouching down beside her.

"An electrostatic print lifter."

"Which is . . . ?"

"You ever notice how dusty your TV screen gets?"

"Sure," Cam answered.

"Televisions produce a high-voltage current that attracts dust. This device uses the same principle to lift impressions. Works best if the impression has some type of dry residue adhering to it."

She took a flat piece of metal from the case. "This is the ground plate, and this"—she held up a black sheet of material—"is polyester film coated on one side with a conductive metal laminate." She carefully lowered the film over the footprint, picked up a metal probe, touched the metalized backing of the film with the probe's tip, and turned on the voltage.

Cam watched with interest as the film flattened tightly against the concrete floor. "The electrical charge causes the impression to record on the film. Right?"

She turned off the voltage. "That's the general idea." She waited a few seconds for the charge to dissipate, then transferred the film to a paper folder and anchored it in place. I'll examine the film in a darkroom, then photograph the impression." She snapped the briefcase closed. "Now, let's go outside and make some casts of the man's thong prints."

After she'd finished pouring the cast mixture into the deep impressions, she picked up her camcorder. "While that's setting, let's check the other greenhouses."

Cam pushed open the door of the adjacent building and gaped. Row after row of camellia, mimosa, magnolia, and jasmine had been jerked from their green plastic pots, then tossed into a pile, the soil dumped onto the floor. "My God!"

"That's what he did to all of the plants in your house."
She started the camcorder. "Can any of these be saved?"

He shook his head sadly. "I don't know, I'll have to
ask the men."

The plants in the next building had also been vandal-
ized. The greenhouses behind and the ones adjacent to
where Gan Haing's body lay had been spared.

Cam and Amy walked toward a long shed where the
workers huddled together. "Why is he doing this, Amy?
What's he after?"

"I don't know. I told you what Hue said about the
men who are terrorizing the townspeople."

"But why target Mai and Chantou?" Tears filmed his
eyes. "Mai never hurt anyone and Chantou was a kind,
peaceable man."

"Our suspect thinks your father-in-law had something
of value. He also thought Mai knew where it was. He
screened most of the loose articles in your house and
took off all the electrical outlet covers, so whatever it is
can't be too large."

"It doesn't make sense. Chantou worked eighteen
hours a day to keep his business going. If he had had
anything of value, wouldn't he have used it to make his
life easier?" He ran a hand across his eyes. "And if Mai
knew, why the hell didn't she tell the man who attacked
her? Why, Amy? Why? Maybe he wouldn't have . . ."

He rested his forehead against the building and beat
his fist on the splintery boards.

Amy put out her hand to comfort him, but before her
fingers touched him, he wheeled around. His face held
no expression, but a wild light burned in his dark eyes.
"I'm going to find him, Amy. I'm going to find him and
kill the son of a bitch the way he killed Mai!"

15

B.J. and Dr. Epps removed Gan Haing's body from the stainless steel autopsy table which Amy immediately sluiced with warm water and wiped dry. When she finished cleaning, she joined the men in the conference room.

Dr. Epps glanced up, his hazel eyes gleaming with excitement. Since he'd watched her father perform Mai's autopsy, he'd become a forensic convert. Today, he'd kept up a steady flow of questions throughout the procedure. "Amy, what do you make of the contusions on his stomach, the back of his neck, and his heels?"

She remembered Nathan taking on a man twice his size. A swift blow to the neck and sternum and the man had collapsed without a sound. "Because both his neck and back were broken, I thought at first that all of them might be from high impact blows. However—"

"Couldn't have been, kitten." B.J. shoved a pad toward her on which he'd drawn several sketches of a man. "His hand had to have been flat on Gan's neck for us to have found the fingerprints. I figure, his assailant got him in a half nelson and rammed his feet onto the concrete. That's about the only way his back could have gotten broken in three places."

Amy shivered. "That would account for the severe contusions on his heels."

Dr. Epps ran his hand over his thinning sandy hair and licked his lips. "The man's heartless. He could have knocked Mr. Haing out and tied him up. He didn't have to kill him."

Amy pulled out a chair and sank into it. While doing the autopsy, she'd thought about Mr. Haing and the life he'd led. Through the years, he'd burned up the fat on his body. The sinew and knobby muscles that remained resembled the roots of wind-ravaged scrub mahogany. Judging from the scars and metal fragments they'd found, he'd gone through great danger before finding his way to Wheeler, where he and his tiny wife had hoped to find peace.

Amy gave a tired sigh and let her shoulders droop. "That man didn't have to rape Mai either—but he did."

Dr. Epps interlaced his fingers. "Fred'll get him." He nodded emphatically. "You folks give him that fingerprint you found on Mr. Haing's neck and Fred'll have him in jail in jig time."

"No, he won't. Our man doesn't have any priors, Homer." B.J. drew black boxes around the edge of his scratch pad. "This is his third murder and we aren't one goddamned bit farther ahead than we were."

Amy stared into space for a moment, then got to her feet. "I'm going to fax a copy of all the fingerprints we've gotten to the FBI. Maybe they can find out if he's ever been in the army." She hesitated, unsure of her father's reaction to her next idea. "I'm also going to send a copy to Nathan."

B.J.'s head snapped up. "What for?"

She met his challenging gaze. "He has special resources."

"You sure that's your only reason?"

"My personal life isn't involved here."

"What's over is over, Amy. Let it go."

She thought of the rage she'd seen in Cam's eyes. No

one except her knew, but tonight he intended to arm himself and patrol the area around the greenhouses. The savage person he sought might torture and kill Cam as he had Mai.

She set her chin in a determined line. "This man has to be stopped before he kills again. I intend to find out who he is. And I don't give a damn what it takes."

Later that evening, Amy lay in bed trying to get to sleep. She remembered the heated discussions she and Nathan had had over their case the previous fall and wished he were here. Perhaps he could think of a new angle, something she hadn't yet pursued.

When there had been the two of them, no obstacle had been too difficult. Suddenly something moved in her abdomen and everything else fled from her mind. Had she imagined that soft flutter? She tensed in an effort to be ready if the feeling came again. Minutes passed and nothing happened. Finally, she let out her breath and let her body go limp. Maybe she'd only imagined it. But then again she experienced the strange surge of movement.

She smiled, hiked up her nightgown, and placed a hand on each side of her abdomen. "Hi, you two," she said softly. "Are you boys or girls?" She chuckled low in her throat. "Or maybe there's one of each. What shall I call you?"

She ran down the list of names she'd been considering. "What if I call you J.B. and J.T. until I know for sure? How's that?" She could have sworn she felt a little wriggle under each palm.

"Are you going to have black hair and eyes like your father, or brown on brown like me?" She grew relaxed and dreamy. "I hope you have his smile." She stretched out her legs and settled her head into a more comfortable position on the pillow and drifted off to sleep.

* * *

First thing the next morning, she called Jed at his office. "Have you heard from Cam?" she asked.

"No, is there any reason why I should?"

"One of Mr. Pran's workmen was killed the night before last."

"Why wasn't I informed?"

"I assumed Cam would call you."

"Well, he didn't. What the hell happened?"

"Our murderer is still searching. He uprooted a bunch of plants and killed the man who works nights at the greenhouse."

"And I suppose the sheriff thinks Cam did it."

"That's right. I'm sure he'd have arrested him if Dad hadn't convinced him that he might be overlooking something that'd cause him bigger trouble later."

"Thank God. How can I reach Cam?"

"I don't know unless there's a phone at the greenhouses. None of his workers would do the night shift, so Cam decided to guard the place himself."

"Good. If he's busy, he won't have so much time to think about Mai."

"I'm worried about him, Jed. He said he was going to get a gun."

"Jesus! You think he's serious?"

"I've never seen him like that before. It was like he became someone else. He's obviously full of rage."

"Will you be going to Wheeler today?"

"No, I have some lab work to do."

"Could you, Amy? I have to be in court all day."

"I guess I could probably get away by noon."

"Thanks. Call me at home this evening."

Amy hurried to her darkroom with the electrostatic

lifting film. What she saw when she looked at it under very low oblique light made her shudder. It couldn't be!

Her fingers shook as she adjusted her camera, took several time shots, and developed the film. As soon as she could get the black and white print out of the fixer, she examined it with a powerful magnifying glass. The sole print was of the right foot, yet it didn't have the triangular scar she'd expected, nor was this person flatfooted.

Carrying the still damp print, she rushed to find her father. She met him as he came out of the lab. "Dad, this footprint isn't from the same man."

He nodded with a gloomy expression. "The FBI just called to say the fingerprints indicate we're dealing with two men."

"Did they have anything on either of them?"

"Nothing."

After discussing the new development in the case, her father left. Amy busied herself with her lab work, but she couldn't keep her mind from wandering. Finally, she gave up and started for Wheeler.

Two men. How did that change the picture? Had both of them come to the house the night Mai was killed? If so one had kept his shoes on. Perhaps Mai had opened the front door for the man she knew and he let the other one in by the back door. Amy shook her head. A person as modest as Mai would never have let someone see her in only a nightgown—even if she knew the man. She would have put on a robe before answering the door.

No . . . Mai heard the door open and got up because she thought it was Cam. She saw the first man and tried to escape by the back door, but the second man was there. He assaulted her, dragged her into the bedroom, tied her up and tortured her while the other man searched the house.

They knew Cam wouldn't walk in on them because

their female accomplice had probably been instructed to call when Cam left her apartment in Seattle.

The faster Amy's mind flew, the faster she drove. She arrived at the greenhouses and learned from one of the elderly gardeners that Cam had gone to Fenwick's for his workout. She breathed a relieved sigh. Perhaps Cam would be able to work off some of his anger.

She drove back into Wheeler. To ensure her car wouldn't be tampered with again, she parked at the curb in the busiest part of the town and walked to the gym.

As she entered the lobby, she caught sight of Cam entering the handball court. When she called to him, he came toward her, his features closed, his manner cool.

She forced a smile. "How about lunch?"

"I'll be on the court for quite awhile."

"That's okay. I have an exercise class, then I can do a few laps in the pool."

Cam's lips tightened. "I'll have to get back to the greenhouse."

"Cam . . ." He reluctantly met her steady gaze. "We have to talk."

He blew out his breath and pointed to a corner furnished with a lamp, three chairs, and some magazines. "I'll meet you there at noon." He turned on his heel and returned to the court.

She noted that his playing companion was Kim, the Asian who had attracted the admiring glances of the women in her class. When he saw her observing her, he smiled and waved.

Her class was assembling as she walked in. "Guess what?" she said as she sat down beside Hue.

Hue rolled her eyes. "Considering what you do, nothing would surprise me."

"I felt the babies kick. Isn't that great?"

Hue looked down at her own protruding abdomen. "Wait until they start working out on the trampoline."

Amy laughed. "That's going to be some feat. I'm carrying twins."

"This your first?"

Amy nodded.

Hue made a face and laughed. "This is my third. I'm glad you're having the twins instead of me." She patted Amy's arm. "They're a lot of work, but they'll make you so happy you'll want more."

Amy placed a hand on each side of her abdomen. *I'll be content with just the two of you*, she thought.

After class, Amy donned a bathing suit and went for a swim. By the time she returned to the dressing room, Hue and the other women had gone home. The walls of the locker room echoed her footsteps as she made her way to and from the shower.

The silent atmosphere made her uneasy and she hurried into her clothes. She had almost finished buttoning her blouse when the lights went out.

She started to call out, but instinct warned her not to. Her gun lay inside her locker across from the bench on which she sat. To get it, she'd have to open the noisy locker door. That would broadcast her exact location. Her heart hammered against her ribs as she felt along the bench until she found her gym sock. Holding it open, she located the bar of soap she'd left to dry and dropped it into the sock. With the sock leg gripped in her hand, she backed against the wall.

No sound. No sound at all, yet she sensed movement. One of the men had used a knife. The other one killed with his hands. She longed to scream, but knew no one would hear her. Panic swelled in her chest. Her breathing quickened. She gulped air. It wasn't enough. As she clutched her throat, she felt the leather thong holding her medicine pouch. Her panic lessened.

Force yourself to be completely still, Nathan had told her. *Center down. Focus on what you see, hear, smell, and feel.* In the pitch darkness she could see nothing, but neither could her assailant. She concentrated on the other three senses.

Although she heard nothing, she felt the air current change around her. The air had a faint, spicy scent of exotic tobacco. Her pulse nearly deafening her, she waited—waited with cold sweat oozing from under her arms—waited until her nose told her where he stood. Then she swung her improvised sap and felt it hit home.

"Bitch!" The sibilant sound ricocheted in the silence. His weapon created a ripple in the air as it plunged and raised again.

Swiftly, she struck again. He cried out and something clattered on the floor. She aimed a kick, felt it land, and lunged for her locker.

"I'll get you, bitch."

She jerked her gun from its holster and whirled around. "Make a move and I'll blow your brains out."

She backed toward the door and scurried into the hall. With the door as a shield, she felt along the inside wall until she found the switch and turned on the lights.

Her pistol ready, she checked the aisles between the lockers and found no one. Somewhere in the dark recesses of the basement, a door slammed. She discovered an exit door in the furnace room behind the showers.

On the cement floor near her locker, she found spots of blood and felt a surge of elation. An instant later, fear overshadowed her triumph. He knew who she was. Maybe he even knew where she lived.

He would try again.

16

Amy charged up the stairs. The exit door she'd found had opened onto the employee's parking lot, but there had been no one in sight. She dashed past the receptionist and scanned the area. How could he have disappeared so quickly?

"How many exits are there in the basement?" she snapped as she studied the few cars in the lot. When Daphne didn't reply, Amy swung around. "Answer me."

The girl stood behind her desk, her eyes big, her face stark white. "Th-Th-Three."

Amy scowled at the girl. "Where?"

"Uh . . . uh . . ."

"Good God, girl—" She raised her hand.

"I'll tell you, I'll tell you. D-Don't shoot . . ."

Amy lowered her arm. "Sorry, I forgot about the gun."

The girl exhaled in relief.

"Look, I'm an investigator." She glanced over and saw that the handball court was empty. "Where are Kim and Dr. Nguyen?"

Daphne shook her head. "Showering?" She answered tremulously.

Amy swallowed. Her assailant could have been Kim. A cold lump gathered in her stomach. *Or even Cam.* He didn't use to smoke, but too many years had passed since their intern days for her to know if he'd taken up the habit.

"Did you see either of them come up the stairs?"

"They could have. I left the desk for about ten minutes."

For the first time in several days, Amy's stomach turned queasy. "Where are the exits, Daphne?"

"One is on the men's side. Another on the women's and the third one is from the pool area."

"Can they be opened from the outside?"

"Yes, but only Mr. Fenwick and a few of the employees have keys."

"But anyone can open them from the inside. Right?"

Daphne nodded.

"Did Dr. Nguyen leave a message for me?"

Daphne moved brochures and papers on her desk. "There's nothing here."

Amy's shoulders slumped. "Thanks. Sorry I frightened you."

She plodded down the stairs, propped the dressing room door open, and collected her things. In the hall, she caught sight of herself as she passed a mirror. Her blouse gaped, her wet hair stuck out at all angles, and her sad eyes looked out of a face with no more color than Daphne's. No wonder the poor girl had been frightened. Amy finished buttoning her blouse, combed her hair, and put on some lipstick.

When she returned to the desk, Amy held her wallet open and showed Daphne her I.D. "How do I get in touch with Mr. Fenwick?" she asked.

"He's in his office." She pointed to a door farther down the lobby.

Amy knocked on the door labeled IVAN FENWICK and walked in. A man who looked to be about forty stood at a counter shoving tomatoes and carrots into a juicer. He wore royal blue sweat pants and a sleeveless T-shirt with the FAC logo. She approached him. "I'm Dr. Amy Prescott."

Bulging deltoids and biceps, which had been tanned a rich brown, rippled as he shut off the machine, poured himself a large paper cupful, and took a sip. "Good stuff." He raised the cup. "Want one? Great for your eyes."

"No, thank you."

He waved her to a chair, sprawled in one across from her, and rested his size-eleven athletic shoes on a coffee table covered with fitness magazines. "Are you interested in becoming a member, Dr. Prescott?"

"I'm trying out one of your classes, but that's not why I'm here."

When she presented her I.D., he took his feet off the table and sat up straight. "Somebody been saying something about my club?" He gulped his drink, crushed the cup into a ball, and hurled it into a green metal wastebasket.

"Not exactly, Mr. Fenwick. Six months ago, the owner of Pran's Landscape Gardens was struck and killed by a hit-and-run driver. The driver was never apprehended. Two weeks ago, Mr. Pran's daughter, Mai Nguyen, was murdered. Yesterday, one of his workmen was killed."

Ivan Fenwick scowled and raked his fingers through his short blond hair. "What's all this got to do with me?" he asked.

"At the scene of the murder we found traces of magnesium carbonate."

Fenwick stared at her, then down at his hands. A white substance edge his cuticles and accentuated the lines in his palms. "So?"

"Since we know weight lifters use the substance, we thought the person who killed Mai might either work here or be a member."

"Nah"—he shook his head—"couldn't be. There's nobody here that'd do a thing like that."

"That's not true, Mr. Fenwick. A week ago, someone punctured my brake line while my car was parked in your lot." She fixed her steady gaze on him. "Today, after my exercise class, I took a swim. When I returned to the dressing room, someone attacked me."

"You mean someone raped you?"

"No. He had a knife; I'm sure he intended to kill me."

Mr. Fenwick leaped to his feet. "I don't believe it." He strode the length of the room and came back to glower down at her. "We've never had anything like that happen here."

Amy stood up. "It's happening now."

Ivan Fenwick crossed his arms over his highly developed pectorals. "The sheriff told me the doctor murdered his wife."

"Cam Nguyen was in jail when my car was tampered with."

"Ah, but he was here today, Doctor." He spread legs the size of tree trunks, put his hands on his hips and thrust out his jaw. "Maybe he figures you're messing in matters better left alone."

"There was another man here today; the man who was playing handball with the doctor."

"You mean Kim Sen. You're way off base, lady. Kim wouldn't hurt a fly."

Amy wrote the name in her notebook and studied it for a moment. Where had she heard that name before? "How long has Mr. Sen worked for you?"

"Eight or nine months."

"What do you know about him?"

"He's a good, reliable worker, gets along with people, and is never late. That's all I need to know."

"What's the name of the Asian who works nights?"

"Victor Samphan. He—" He halted abruptly. "Now wait a minute. I don't want to get anyone in trouble."

"We've already eliminated your Caucasian employees. If we can do the same with the two Asians, you're in the clear. Have you had some trouble with Victor?"

"He's got a short fuse. Gets mean when he drinks. Knocks his kids and old lady around. He's been jailed a few times. But I sure as hell don't think he'd get mixed up in a murder."

"I used to work at the crime lab in Seattle. I saw terrible things committed by people who didn't appear to be the type. Do both of your men have keys to the exit doors of the club?"

"Yes."

"Would you give me their addresses?"

"Well, I might"—Fenwick rubbed the back of his neck and narrowed his eyes at her—"if you agree to forget the assault. News like that can ruin a club." He smiled and gestured to a chair. "Let's relax and talk about it."

Amy sat down. "I do intend to find the man. Make no mistake about that, Mr. Fenwick."

"Make that Ivan, Dr. Prescott. And you're welcome to use the club facilities any time you'd like."

"I doubt if I'll be spending much time in Wheeler once this case is closed. However, any mention I might make about your club shouldn't endanger your business."

"Fine. Fine. Glad to hear it." Ivan beamed at her, got to his feet, pulled out a drawer, and handed her two time cards.

The gardeners at the greenhouse told Amy that Cam hadn't returned and they didn't know where he was staying. Amy left a note for him with the head gardener telling him they were dealing with two men instead of just one. She warned him to use caution since the men might think he knew the location of the item they sought. She closed with a plea for him to call her or Jed.

With that out of the way, she consulted the information Ivan Fenwick had given her. Kim's address led her to a two-story clapboard building with faded white paint. The landlady who presided over the rooming house either didn't speak English or didn't want Amy to know that she did.

Amy studied the cars at the curb. If either Kim or Victor was the culprit, it was possible that one of them owned the blue pickup that followed her the first day she'd visited Cam at the jail.

She drove up the alley behind the rooming house and came upon several old cars and an ancient gray van. HANUMAN JANITORIAL SERVICE was hand-painted in uneven letters on the van's rust-streaked panels. Amy wrote down the name and the license numbers of the cars and went on her way.

The quest for Victor Samphan led her to a remote wooded canyon. Through thick stands of fir, she caught glimpses of the turbulent water of the Wasku River. After following a mud-slick lane for several miles, she located Samphan's house. Set back in a grove of cedars, it was scarcely visible from the road.

When Amy knocked, a woman opened the door only wide enough for her slender body to slip through. She appeared to be in her late twenties or early thirties, yet her face looked drawn and haggard.

"Hello," Amy said, and smiled at her. The woman's dark eyes remained wide with fear. "Are you Mrs. Samphan?" she asked.

When the woman nodded nervously, Amy asked, "Is your husband at home?"

The woman shook her head. "No, he's not here."

"Perhaps I could wait. Do you expect him back soon?"

The woman twisted cracked, reddened fingers together. "I don't know." She moistened her lips. "Probably two or three hours. He—he's very seldom home. He works two jobs."

"I see." Amy gave her a business card. "Please have him call me. I want to ask him a few questions."

The woman nodded and closed the door.

Amy slogged through the mud to her car. A whole day lost and nothing gained. When she happened to glance behind her, she glimpsed a man watching her from around a corner of the house.

Then she spied the blue pickup in the shed.

17

"Shit!"

Jed's expletive traveled through the receiver with such force it hurt her ear. "Getting angry won't help, Jed."

"I don't give a damn. Do you think Cam's carrying a gun?"

"Could be. I tried to argue him out of getting one the other day. That could be why he's avoiding me."

"Jesus, I hope he doesn't screw around and get himself in worse trouble than he already is."

"He's like a different person."

"A man whose wife has been brutally raped and murdered changes, Amy. I'll take a run over there tomorrow and see if I can find him. Let me know if he calls you."

Amy hung up the receiver and went to look out the living room window. Rain sprayed the glass and droplets drizzled down the slick surface. In the muted glow of the lamppost, she could see water overflowing the gutters. Cars created geysers as they plowed through hub-deep pools.

Cam could be out patrolling the greenhouses in this deluge, she thought. Anything could happen. He wasn't used to such hardships. What would he do if confronted by Mai's assailants? He was a doctor, not a fighter. She doubted if he even knew how to defend himself.

She rinsed and dried the few dishes she'd used for dinner. When alone, she seldom felt justified in using the dishwasher. When she'd given the kitchen a thorough cleaning, she moved on to the living room. There she straightened stacks of forensic science journals on the dark oak coffee table, and fluffed the cinnamon, gold, and loden green velvet pillows decorating the glide rocker and the toffee-colored couch.

All the while she worked, she sensed an underlying desperation in her attempt to put her house in order. She refused to let herself consider the source.

By eleven o'clock she had run out of excuses to stay up, so she put on a flannel shirt that had belonged to Nathan and went to bed. She seldom wore the shirt for fear it'd lose his scent, but tonight she feared she might need the comfort the shirt gave her.

The instant she turned out the light, fear clutched her chest. Again, she stood in the basement of the gym straining to see the killer. Would he come at her with his hands, or his knife? Perspiration broke out on her body and she fought for breath.

The sharp shrilling of her bedside phone jerked her back to reality. Her heart still pounding rapidly, she snatched up the receiver. "Hel-Hello?" She stammered. Her voice sounded shrill and breathless to her ears.

"I had to know that you were all right."

"Nathan . . ." She gulped for air.

"Sorry I woke you."

"You didn't."

"Amy, I know this is wrong. But I got that awful feeling about you again today and I was afraid that . . . Are you sure you're all right?"

She hadn't told her father or Jed about the attack—
How could he have known? To avoid answering the
question, she changed the subject. "I'm glad you called.
I needed to talk to you."

"What about?"

"I mailed you copies of the fingerprints we have.
AFIS has nothing on the two men."

"There are two?"

"Yes. One of them was in one of the pictures you
took when you were in the Asian vegetable market."

"Send me an enlarged print."

"I will. Remember the piece of caramel candy I
found by the fir tree? The dentist says the man has a
broken front tooth. And the man who was watching me
the day I was at Cam's house does too."

"You didn't mention anything about such a man the
last time we talked."

She took a quick breath. "I must have forgotten. Anyway, one or the other or both ransacked Pran's greenhouse. Uprooted a bunch of plants. He killed one of the
gardeners. Broke his neck and back."

There was a silence before Nathan finally said, "I
thought they might be Khmer Rouge."

"What? This isn't Cambodia."

"The FBI have had reports of them infiltrating Asian
communities in the U.S."

"The man who saw the driver who hit Mr. Pran re-
ferred to him as one of the *yavana*. He refused to identify him."

"Smart man. They would kill him and his family."

"An Asian woman I met says they're extorting
money from the shopkeepers. Do you think they're the
same men who killed Mai?"

"Their methods are similar, but that doesn't mean much."

"How am I to solve a crime when everyone is frightened to tell me anything?"

"Whatever you do, be careful, Amy. I have seen the awful things these men do to women. I fear for you."

For an instant, she was back in the dark locker room again. "So do I. I don't even trust Cam anymore. I—I . . . Oh, Nathan, I wish you were here.'"

He let out a long sigh. "I wish I were too."

She swallowed a lump in her throat. "I know it would only make things worse for you."

"Impossible. My life is already a mess. In the four months I've been married, I've slept with my wife once, and that was on our wedding night."

Amy felt as if her jaws had locked and it hurt to force out words. "Why is that?"

"I don't know. When I try to talk to her, she cries and begs me not to leave her."

Amy didn't want to hear about their problems, didn't want to feel sorry for a woman who stood between her and the man she loved. "Have you tried a counselor?"

"Angela refuses. Worse yet, I have no way of knowing if her problems are because of something I did or something I did not do." He sighed. "I shouldn't ask you this, Amy, but I have to know. Was I a good lover?"

"Nathan . . ."

"Please, Amy, tell me. Did I give you pleasure?"

If he had cut out her heart, she couldn't have hurt any worse. Still, she couldn't deny him the reassurance he needed. "No one has ever made me feel as you did. I—I didn't even know I was capable of experiencing such . . . of feeling like that."

"Neither did I, *Mihewi*. When I am with you, I have"—he cleared his throat—"*spirit* feelings . . . My people call it *liloiz gaudeo,* causing joy."

Amy was silent, not knowing how to respond.

"Then, there is the other feeling," Nathan continued. He laughed softly. "You smile, or flip your hair, or flash your eyes at me and my heart thunders. I think, I must touch her. And when I do"—his voice grew husky— "*Mihewi*, my Sun Woman, *heteuit*, my blood turns to fire and I want you."

"I know."

"You feel that way *too?*"

"Yes."

"*Mihewi . . .*" He hesitated for a long moment. "Amy, would you have made love with me the last time I saw you?"

"Yes."

He chuckled. "Right there in your conference room?"

Her laughter had a bittersweet quality about it. "On the chair, on the table, on the floor. It wouldn't have mattered to me."

"Or to me." He drew in a deep breath, then let it out. "Describe your bedroom. I want to picture you there."

She smiled, thinking of him imagining her. "The wallpaper is cream-colored with little yellow roses. The curtains and spread are white with lace trim."

"What do you have on?"

She laughed. "Your flannel shirt."

"My shirt! I thought you would be wearing something pink and filmy I could see through."

"I have some of those too, but at special times I wear your shirt because it comforts me."

"Amy, how can you forgive me for what I have done to you?"

"You did what you thought was right at the time." She gave a weary sigh. "And that, I'm afraid, is a lot more praiseworthy than what we're doing now."

18

The next morning, as Amy was dressing, the twins made her aware of their presence again. "Good morning, babies," she said, somewhat self-conscious at hearing her voice in the quiet room. Recently she'd read that pregnant women should talk and sing to their unborn babies. Researchers claimed an unborn child had thoughts and feelings and might even sense its mother's moods. Since that was the case, she decided she'd sing and talk regardless of who might think she'd slipped a cog. Besides, it made the twins seem more real and helped ease her loneliness.

"So, J. T. and J. B.," she said in a cheerful tone. "I guess it's about time I started thinking about getting a nanny."

She took a pencil and scratch pad into the kitchen and wrote, *Wanted: Live-in Nanny,* at the top of the page, then stirred rolled oats into water and started the microwave. *Motherly woman,* In her mind, she envisioned a plump, large-bosomed woman of around fifty.

Amy dropped two slices of bread into the toaster and scribbled, *Must love children.* When the toast popped up, she buttered it and sat down to eat. "You guys are certainly changing your mother's life. Before you came along, I seldom thought of food. Now look at me." She laughed. "One way or another, you're going to turn me into a blimp."

After she finished eating, she took her scratch pad with her and went downstairs to the lab. "I'm going to advertise for a live-in nanny," she said to her father, who was sitting on a stool reading a computer printout of her notes.

"Why now? You won't need one for five months."

"I'm going to need a labor coach."

"Your Aunt Helen or I could do that."

"No, I want to get to know whoever will be taking care of the twins. I need to know what she's like, how she reacts in times of stress." She pulled the pad toward her. Even though she knew she had little hope of finding such a person, she added, *Would prefer someone who speaks the Nez Perce tongue and knows their customs.*

With that matter taken care of, she slipped two prepared glass slides under separate objectives of the comparison microscope and adjusted the focus. One slide contained cotton fibers taken from a bedpost at the Nguyen house, the other a sample from the rope they'd found hidden in the woods.

As flat fibers resembling twisted ribbon came into view, she swore under her breath. Although aware that white cotton can be found in almost any sample of house dust, she had still hoped her samples might be unique.

She removed the slides and tossed them in the disposal can. "No luck. The rope is useless as evidence unless you found some blood or tissue on it."

B. J. glanced up. "No. Not a thing that's of any help."

She set up the upholstery samples she'd clipped from the furniture of the apartment where Cam claimed he'd met with Chea Le and compared them with fibers she'd found on Cam's clothing. Finally, she let out a heavy breath. "Doesn't look like Cam was ever in apartment 105."

"You can't be positive, kitten. They might have changed the furniture." He pointed to the printout. "Who are Kim Sen and Victor Samphan?"

"Employees of Fenwick's Athletic Club." She checked through the other labeled slides to see if she'd examined all the specimens. "Ivan Fenwick gave me their addresses yesterday. One man drives a blue pickup. Couldn't get his license number, but I did list a few other licenses you might run through AFIS."

"Will do. Why don't you rest today? You're looking a bit pale."

She and Nathan had talked for two hours the previous night, so she hadn't slept much, but she couldn't tell her father that. "Probably anemia. The doctor says mothers of twins may lose more iron."

"Double trouble." He shook his head. "God help us if they turn out to be as stubborn as you are."

She smiled wryly. "Takes one to know one, Dad."

The ringing of the phone cut off his retort. She lifted the receiver. "Good morning. This is Dr. Amy Prescott."

"Amy, this is Hue. I had to call you . . . Oh, goodness—the most awful thing . . . wait until you hear—"

"Hue, what is it?"

The woman swallowed noisily. "My husband works for the county road department. The river's over its banks. The guys have been watching the bridges for log jams. This morning they found a car. A—A blue Honda, Amy, and—and there's a dead woman in it."

Amy's pulse started to race. "Hold on a second, Hue." She turned to her father. "Wheeler. They found a car in the river with a body inside."

B. J. hopped off his stool and crossed over to her.

Amy raised the receiver to her ear again. "Is she Asian?"

"I don't know. My husband said they haven't identified her yet."

"Did anyone call the police?"

"My husband doesn't like Sheriff Boyce, Amy. He said to let you know first."

"Thanks, Hue. Where's the car?"

"They towed it into a field near the Wasku River bridge."

"Fine. Give us a twenty-minute head start, then call the sheriff. He shouldn't be able to do too much damage before we get there."

Hue giggled. "Gee, Amy, I feel as if I'm in a TV mystery."

"Good job, Sergeant Quoy," Amy said with a laugh. "I'll get back to you with a full report this evening."

19

Amy and B.J. each took their own vehicles to the scene.

Amy floor-boarded the accelerator as she left Ursa Bay's city limits. If the dead woman was Chea Le, the sheriff might blame Cam. She wanted to prevent that from happening, if she could.

Before leaving, she'd called Jed's office. His secretary said he'd left for Wheeler two hours ago. Amy issued up a prayer that he'd found Cam and straightened out his thinking.

Amy crested a hill, caught a brief glimpse of the flooded valley. After rounding several switchbacks, she reached the floor of the canyon and crossed the Wasku River bridge. The road department had towed the blue Honda onto higher ground.

She parked on a logging byway beside Sheriff Boyce's car and prepared to change from shoes to rubber boots. Off to her right, a sturdily built Asian of medium height was controlling the gathering crowd, edging onlookers back behind a strip of yellow crime tape. Deputy Pierce waved along rubbernecking motorists.

He loped over and pounded on her window. "Move it, lady. You can't park here."

Amy finished jamming on her boot and rolled down her window. "Deputy Pierce, the body has to be examined before the car can be moved."

He shoved his thick-lensed glasses into place with a muddy forefinger. "That's not my problem. Now move it."

Amy closed the window, tucked her slacks into the tops of her boots, and got out of the car. "I'll go clear it with the sheriff, how's that?"

"Piss off, Prescott." The deputy kicked her tire. "I'm running this show."

Her father's van rolled to a stop behind hers and he hopped out. "Something wrong, Amy?"

"Deputy Pierce thinks it's a problem that we're parked here."

As he spoke, Homer Epps pulled up in his minivan. He slammed the door and joined them. "I'm not looking forward to this task," he said. He turned and patted Deputy Pierce on the arm. "Keep an eye on our cars will you, son?"

"God damn it to hell, Homer."

Dr. Epps smiled and patted him again. "Thanks, Duane, you're a good boy."

He turned to B.J. who'd slid open the side of his van and was assembling his equipment on the ground. "Anything I can help you carry, B.J.?"

B.J. gestured toward the aluminum gurney and the tote case that held his battery-powered work lights, then glanced at the gray sky. "I hope this weather holds. This job will be tough enough without fighting the rain."

He slid the van door closed and hoisted his forensic gear. "Need any help, Amy?"

Amy slung the straps of her purse and two camera straps around her neck. "No, you go on ahead. I want to talk to Hue's husband."

Carrying her forensic satchel, she stepped off the graveled strip where they'd parked. She slogged through ankle-deep water to a man in an orange workman's jacket who was taking in the scene. "Excuse me, are you Raymond Quoy?"

"That's me." His round face crinkled into laugh lines. "Are you Dr. Prescott?" At her nod, his smile broadened. "Me and the kids have been hearing 'Amy this' and 'Amy that' ever since Hue met you."

Amy laughed. "She and I have a mutual admiration pact. I think very highly of your wife, Mr. Quoy."

"So do I." He flushed and glanced at her out of the corner of his eye. "And call me Raymond, everybody else in town does."

She nodded. "Raymond, have you or any of the other men seen that car before?"

"I haven't." He gazed down at his mud-splashed boots. "Some of my men may have." His eyes met hers. "But I don't want Sheriff Boyce to know that. The men are scared they might end up like she did."

"Do you think any of them knew her?"

"No one mentioned any names."

"Was the car full of water?"

"Yes. All four windows were open several inches."

"Did you notice if the body was on the driver's or passenger's side of the car?"

"She was behind the steering wheel. The seat belt was holding her in place."

"Thanks, Raymond, you've been a big help."

"She looks pretty awful, Dr. Prescott." He grimaced. "I wouldn't want to do what you do."

"That's what most people say." She smiled. "You better call me Amy, or Hue won't know who you're talking about."

He reached for her satchel. "Let me take that for you," he said.

Amy started to decline his offer, but he'd already taken the bag. She was glad he had. To reach the car, they had to travel through stretches of heavy mud, tall grass, and weeds that dragged at her feet. When she reached the scene, she thanked Raymond for his assistance.

He lifted his orange cap by the bill, said, "Nice to have met you," and went back to join his men.

Amy walked over to where her father and Dr. Epps were at work. The car sat on a ridge at bottom of a shale-covered slope. B.J. had divided the exterior of the car into quadrants and assigned a portion to Dr. Epps. B.J. examined the car's bumper and grill with a magnifying glass.

He glanced at Amy. "Take lots of pictures."

"Stupid waste of time." Sheriff Boyce stood with his gaze angled away from the car. He kicked a rock into the water and flung out his arms. "Jesus Christ! There ain't no sense in going through this whole damned rigmarole again."

"Why is that, Sheriff?" Amy kept a smile pasted on her face. She wanted to keep their conversation on an amiable level if she possibly could. Perhaps, if he had time to think something through he might not jump to one of his screw-loose conclusions.

The sheriff stared out at the churning floodwaters. "The woman was probably drunk, or speeding, or both, and went into the river."

B.J. snorted derisively. "Both the front and rear license plates are gone."

"That's right, Fred." Dr. Epps shifted his attention from the right rear fend to Sheriff Boyce. "Seems to me someone doesn't want us to know who she is."

Sheriff Boyce swung around, caught sight of the body, and turned pale. He looked as though he might vomit. "They coulda gotten snagged on something," he finally said in a weak voice.

Dr. Epps' gaze darted from Amy to B.J. When neither of them commented, he said, "It's possible, I guess."

Amy busied herself adjusting her camera and snapping pictures. If she got pulled into their discussion, she'd lose her patience for sure.

"Bumper and grill are unmarked and intact." B.J., with an obstinate expression, flung the declaration at the sheriff's back. "Pretty damned hard to run off a road without hitting something." He inspected the windows and door handles, dusted and searched for prints.

Dr. Epps peered at B.J. from around the back of the car. "How're we going to get inside with all the doors locked?"

"I have a Slim Jim." B.J.'s eyes twinkled. "You want to jimmy the door lock, Sheriff?"

Sheriff Boyce glanced over his shoulder and gave him a sour look. "No way. Dead people give me the willies."

B.J. worked the device, opened the door, and stepped aside while Amy drew a rough sketch of the inside and the position of the corpse. Dr. Epps stood in the background, observing her.

A smile twitched the corners of Amy's mouth. If his interest held, he'd soon be a much more efficient coroner. She photographed the car's interior, indicating the angle of each shot on her sketch.

Behind her, B.J. fidgeted with impatience. "Is the key in the ignition?"

"Yes. In the off position."

"How about the light switch?"

Amy snapped another picture. "That's off too. And the gear shift is in neutral."

Dr. Epps cleared his throat. "The ignition would have been on and the car in gear," he said, raising his voice. "If the woman went into the river by accident."

B.J. nodded. "That's right. How about the emergency brake, Amy?"

She squatted down to get a clearer view. "It's not engaged, and there's no registration slip on the steering post."

"Could be in the glove compartment," B.J. tested the dead woman's seat belt. "This is sure cinched up tight."

Amy noticed a clamp on the seat belt similar too those used to hold a child seat in place. "Better make sure of the distance from her feet to the pedals before you move her."

"Good idea." B.J. took the measurements while Amy recorded them on her sketch.

After he finished, Amy moved in to fasten paper sacks around the woman's hands and feet. In the meantime, B.J. and Dr. Epps arranged an unzipped body bag on the gurney. As soon as Amy completed her task, the two men tackled the chore of getting the corpse out of the car.

"This isn't something I'd want to do every day," Dr. Epps said as he slid his arm under the woman's knees.

"We're lucky the water was so damned cold. It

slowed decomposition." B.J. grasped the woman's shoulders. "Ready?"

Dr. Epps nodded and together, they got her out of the car and into the body bag.

The instant B.J. closed the zipper, the sheriff strode over and peered in the car's side window. "Her purse is on the floor in the rear of the car. That'll tell us who she is." He reached out to grab the door handle.

Amy opened her mouth to object, then remembered she was in a subordinate position at the scene. "Don't you think I'd better dust it for prints first?"

The sheriff snatched back his hand. "Well, get to it. What the hell you waiting for?"

After making a note of the purse's location, Amy got out her fingerprint kit. A light brush of gray powder on both sides of the black patent leather clutch bag revealed nothing but an unblemished surface. She handed it to the sheriff. "It's been wiped clean."

Boyce thrust out his chin. "Bull."

"Any woman who owns a patent leather purse can tell you they are usually covered with fingerprints."

Sheriff Boyce growled and unclasped the bag. Inside were a lipstick, a mascara, a comb, and several dimes. "Shit!" He flung the bag on the backseat, stormed around the car, jerked open the passenger door and punched in the button on the glove box. It contained a sodden Washington State map and an owner's guide. He slammed the car door harder than necessary, folded his arms, and surveyed them with beetled brows.

"Are your men going to tow the car to impound?" B.J. asked.

"I sure as hell can't leave it here."

"Fine," B.J. said. "We'll meet them there and go over the interior."

He grabbed hold of his end of the gurney. "Lead off, Homer."

Sheriff Boyce wheeled on Amy. "*He* did this, didn't he? That's how come you and your old man know what's happening in Wheeler sooner than anybody else does."

Amy bristled. "Who're you talking about?" she said, though she knew perfectly well who Boyce was accusing.

He narrowed his eyes and moved forward a step. "Your gook friend. That's who."

Anger heated her cheeks. "*Dr. Nguyen* is—"

"Doctor, hell. He's a killer, that's what he is." His spittle sprayed her face. "Where is he?"

Amy clenched her fist until her nails bit into her palm. "He's where he should be," she said in as even a tone as she could manage. "He's taking care of his father-in-law's landscape business."

"*His* business, you mean. That's one more reason he had to kill his wife." He stomped off toward his car. "He's going back to jail, Prescott, and no hotshot lawyer's gonna get him out."

Amy glared at his stiff-necked figure, picked up as much of the equipment as she could carry, and followed the men along the graveled logging road. She'd gone only a short way when she spotted Jed MacManus hurrying toward her.

"What the hell's going on?" he yelled before he had even reached her.

Amy set down her burden. "Did you find Cam?"

"Missed him, goddammit. He was out at the greenhouses last night." Jed shook his head. "This morning he got a phone call and took off." He gestured toward B.J. and Dr. Epps. "Who's in the bag?" he said.

"An Asian woman. They found her car in the river this morning."

"Is she the one we're looking for?"

She shrugged. "No I.D. of any kind. Registration and license plates were gone."

"Anybody recognize her?"

"That wouldn't be easy. The car's been in the river for a week or more."

A worried look spread over Jed's face. "What's the sheriff so burned up about?"

"He thinks Cam's responsible."

Jed shoved his hands into the pockets of his blue down jacket. "God, Amy, he wouldn't skip town, would he?"

Amy felt a stab of fear. "He's an emotional wreck, Jed. He's angry and impatient and he may have a gun." Her sense of foreboding increased with each word she spoke. "He's capable of anything."

20

Despite the nagging pain in her back, Amy persevered. She and B.J. removed the Honda's rear seat. A large stain had soaked into the upholstery. They planned to dry it slowly at the lab before running any tests.

They dried all surfaces inside the car with hair driers, rolled up the windows, and used cyanoacrylate as a fuming agent.

They inspected every portion of the interior. As B.J. squatted on his haunches in the back, he sighed. "Dammit, this guy was too blasted careful. Everything's clean."

"Keep looking. Even the cleverest killers make mistake." Amy eased herself onto the floor of the front seat until she lay on her side. She shone her flashlight this way and that, straining her neck to see into nooks and crannies. Finally, she let out a yell. "Found one on the seat adjustment lever." She rolled over onto her back and peered upward. "There are a couple others on the underside of the steering wheel."

"Good. While you're finishing here, I'm going to start packing up. I want to get done and go home. I'm pooped."

Half an hour later, they were getting ready to leave when Sheriff Boyce's car splashed down the flood-eroded street leading to the fenced impound lot and came to a mud spurting stop.

He got out of the car and marched over to them. "I've turned this whole goddamned town upside down." He glared at Amy. "That slant-eyed sonofabitch has disappeared."

Amy glared back. "Watch your mouth, Sheriff. I've had all I can take of your bigoted slurs."

B.J. placed a gentle hand on her shoulder. "Why are you looking for Dr. Nguyen?"

The sheriff's face turned red and blotchy with anger. "He's given me all the grief he's going to. That's why. I'm putting out a warrant for his arrest."

"Don't you think that's a bit premature? We haven't found a shred of evidence to indicate Cam had anything to do with this woman's death."

"He knew her, didn't he?"

"We have to prove who she is before we'll know that."

The sheriff snorted. "Don't pull that crap on me, Prescott. You two probably been hiding stuff just to protect the sneaky bastard." He turned on his heel, got into his car and sped away.

Dusk had fallen by the time B.J. and Amy got their evidence pouches sorted, recorded, and stowed away in their lab. B.J. patted Amy on the shoulder. "Go get some rest, kitten. You look beat."

She took the elevator upstairs to her apartment, called Hue, then flopped onto the couch and propped her swollen feet on a stack of pillows.

In spite of her weariness, questions battered her brain. Where was Cam? Why had he run off? Was the dead woman Chea Le? If so, who had killed her and why?

The phone she'd placed on the coffee table rang, interrupting her thoughts. She lifted the receiver and answered.

"God, Amy," Jed said. "You sound like I feel."

"Four deaths, Jed. And we still don't have any answers. It's getting me down."

"Me too. Have you eaten dinner?"

"I haven't had the energy."

"Let's go somewhere. Maybe we'll think better on a full stomach."

She sighed. "Sounds nice, but I don't feel up to it."

"Then I'll bring it to you. Do you like Chinese?"

Tears sprang into her eyes, almost taking her by surprise. "Yes, but Jed—"

"You live on Endicott don't you?"

"I'm not fit company for—"

"—anyone but me," he finished for her. "I'll be there in an hour. Okay?"

"I suppose so. Ring the bell and I'll let you in."

She dragged herself into the bathroom, washed her face, combed her hair, and dabbed on lipstick. Her efforts failed to make her feel any less miserable.

She stared at herself in the mirror. *Jed can't take Nathan's place.* The tears came again. She squeezed her eyes shut. *How long? How long before the hurt and despair turned to bitterness?*

She walked through the apartment in her stocking feet, switching on lights and putting the rooms in order. When the buzzer sounded, she pushed a button and spoke into the intercom, "What's the password?"

Jed chuckled. "A closed mouth gathers no feet."

Amy laughed and was amazed at how much better it made her feel. She triggered the downstairs lock and a few minutes later heard the clang of the elevator's brass grilled gate as Jed got out on the second floor. She hurried to open the door.

Jed carried two large brown paper sacks that issued forth the distinct aroma of chow mein. "Where do you want this?"

"Let's eat in the kitchen." She led him into a room where farm scene wallpaper complemented oak floors and cabinetry.

"This is nice," Jed said, setting the bags on the counter. "I like early American." He grinned. "Makes me feel like I'm at my grandmother's house."

"Me too," she said, making a face at him. "I patterned it after my father's kitchen on Lomitas Island. The house belonged to my great, great, great grandparents."

Jed opened the cardboard containers of food while she set two place settings on the round oak table's gingham plaid cloth. "How did you know where I lived?"

"Cam told me once. Why?"

"We don't give out our address. You never know when someone you've helped convict might come looking for you."

He nodded grimly. "That's the excuse my ex-wife gave for not having children."

She looked across the table at him. "She had a point. I've been worrying about it ever since I got pregnant."

"But you still would have gotten pregnant. Right?"

She took a breath and let it out. "Under different circumstances, I would have timed it a little better. But, yes, I wanted a child." She bit her lip. Not just *a* child— Nathan's child.

She moved to the sink. "Do you want tea?" She filled a copper kettle, set it on the stove, and turned on the burner.

"No, thanks." He pulled a bottle of wine from one of the sacks. "I need something to make me forget what a lousy day this has been. Got a cork puller?"

She dug out a corkscrew she'd purchased at a wine tasting party at the Chateau St. Michelle vineyard. The sight of the stainless steel object evoked unpleasant memories of the final days of her marriage. Mitch had gotten high at the party and made passes at every woman in the room.

Pushing aside thoughts of the quarrel that had ensued, she took a goblet and a cup from the cupboard and set them on the table.

"Would you like a glass, Amy?"

"Alcohol is off limits."

"Oh, of course." Jed continued to work the gadget's metal prongs down each side of the cork. "So, do you have any idea where Cam might have gone?"

"I have a list of his acquaintances. You might give them a call."

He popped the cork, filled his glass, and took a long sip. "His jumping bail sure as hell won't help his court case."

"Neither will anything else that's happened lately." Amy put a spoon in each container, set them on the table, and sat down. "It's time we got a break of some kind."

"You said you were going to check the clothing Cam wore the night of the murder. Find anything?"

"Nothing that matched the upholstery in the apartment he claims he was in."

Jed blew out his breath, helped himself to a portion of

beef with Chinese mushrooms and bamboo shoots, and passed the box to Amy. "Did you learn anything more about the dead woman?"

"No. The person responsible made sure of that. I did find three good fingerprints. Maybe they'll tell us something."

"How long has she been dead?"

Amy regarded him with a half smile. "Are you sure you want to discuss this while you're eating?"

Jed laughed and spooned Kung Pao shrimp onto his plate. "Maybe not."

When the kettle on the stove began to whistle, he jumped up, filled the teapot, and set it on a wrought iron trivet beside her. When he'd stood silently at her side for some moments, she glanced up to find him gazing down at her with a soft expression. "God, you smell good."

Oh, hell. "Is that a friend-to-friend remark or . . . what?"

He brushed his knuckle along her cheek. "What if it was a let's-get-friendlier remark?"

"I'd say you'd better sit down and eat your dinner."

"I was afraid of that." He walked back around the table and sat down. "Okay, what about those Asians who work at the athletic club?"

"My friend Hue says that one of them, Victor Samphan, likes to gamble."

"Hmm." Jed sipped his wine. "I wonder if he owes some of our suspects money?"

"Interesting thought." Amy dunked boneless chicken into black bean sauce. "I think he may be the one who was following me."

Jed set down the wine bottle he'd lifted to refill his

glass and regarded her with concern. "You didn't tell me someone was following you."

She shrugged and served herself some Chinese greens. "I was also attacked in the athletic club basement."

"For Christ's sake, Amy," Jed exclaimed, his eyes blazing. "Do you think you take enough chances?"

"Things happen, Jed."

He raised his glass. "Yeah, to you they do. *All the time.*"

She raised an eyebrow. "Lighten up, Jed. He's not likely to try it again."

"Why the hell not?"

"Cause he found out I'm not easy prey." She lay her hand over his. "But thank you for caring."

He clasped her hand in both of his. "I think about you." His brows knotted and he scowled down at the table. "I don't want to, but I do." He lifted his gaze to meet hers. "I can't help wondering what it would be like to—"

"Hold it, Jed." She pulled her hand free. "You said you needed a friend."

"I know, but—"

"No buts. That's all I'll ever be."

"Because you're going to be true to the bastard who got you pregnant and married another woman? Is that it?"

Heat flared in her cheeks. "He doesn't know."

His eyes widened. "Doesn't know? What are you going to tell him when he finds out?"

She leaned forward, her eyes boring into his. "He isn't *going* to find out." She narrowed her eyes. "Not ever. Is that clear, Jed?"

"Amy." He ran his hand over his face. "A woman in

your condition shouldn't be alone, doesn't need to be alone. Yet you've chosen to isolate yourself. What made you decide to have the babies in the first place?"

Amy's throat tightened and her voice was low when she spoke. "Because it's better to have a flesh and blood reminder than nothing at all."

"You loved him that much?"

She lifted her chin. "Love him," she corrected.

"He's a lucky bastard, then, even if he doesn't know it."

She started to reply, but her lip began to tremble.

Jed got up and walked around the table. "Come here." He raised her to her feet and put his arms around her. "If you ever need a hug, I'm here for you."

Amy felt the twins move inside her and she let out a soft "Ohh."

Jed drew away from her, his eyes wide. "Was that what I think it was?"

"They get kind of lively at times."

Jed smiled and eyed her stomach. "Okay, kids, I'll try not to encroach on your papa's territory." His eyes lingered on her face. "But I can't promise. Your Mom is just too damn sweet and lovely."

21

Amy wheeled the gurney from the morgue at 5:00 A.M. She shot photographs of the body clothed and naked, then weighed and measured her. The woman had a small frame, weighed ninety-two pounds, and was fifty-six inches tall.

Donning a lead apron, Amy took several x-rays. After putting the film in the processor, she returned to the body. Both of the woman's hands were tightly clenched. With some difficulty, she straightened the fingers of the right hand. Inside, she found a triangular scrap of royal blue fabric with a white shirt button attached.

She stowed the material away in an evidence bag before assembling the equipment she would need for fingerprinting. The victim's skin, wrinkled from having been immersed in water for so long, would make the procedure difficult. Nevertheless, she was grateful the extremely cold temperature of the river had kept the tissues in a helpful state of preservation.

She tried several methods without satisfactory results. Finally, she injected silicone to round out the finger pads and took photographs before inking the woman's fingers and getting prints. As she took them, she silently chanted the mantra: *Please be on file somewhere.*

She was just finishing when Dr. Epps and her father entered through the back door.

"Morning, Amy," Dr. Epps greeted her, then went to study the corpse.

B.J. ambled over to where Amy stood and read her notes as she recorded the work she'd done on the log sheet. "Why didn't you stay in bed? You wore yourself out yesterday."

"Today's post will be a lengthy one, Dad. I wanted to get the prelims out of the way."

"Did you hang her clothing to dry?"

"Yes."

Clearing his throat, he gazed at the ceiling and rocked from his heels to his toes. "So, did you, uh, have company last night?"

Amy smiled to herself. The windows of his apartment overlooked the street the same as hers did. "Uh-huh." She continued to write.

He coughed and jingled the change in his pocket. "Thought the car looked kind of like the one that lawyer of Cam's was driving yesterday."

"Oh yes?"

"Personable young man."

"I suppose."

"Seems quite taken with you."

"Possibly."

"You . . . could do worse you know."

"Perhaps."

She thought about mentioning Jed's recent divorce, but knew it wouldn't put an end to her father's meddling.

"Unfortunately I'm not interested." She returned the log clipboard to its hook on the wall.

"There are times when I wish you weren't so damned independent."

She grinned at him. "Then you wouldn't have anyone to fight with." She took his arm. "Let's go look at the X-rays."

She retrieved the dried film from the bin where the processor had deposited them, carried them into the next room, and arranged them on the bank of fluorescent view boxes.

Dr. Epps and B.J. gathered around her. "Look at the costochondral junctions." Dr. Epps tapped the rib cage.

"Yep," B.J. said and walked down the line of view boxes, peering at the X-rays of the corpse's arms and legs. "Notice the lower ends of the radius, ulna, tibia, and fibula."

Amy ranged back and forth. "Yes, she definitely has all the indications of childhood rickets, including the pigeon breast and the bowed leg bones. Must have given her some problems. Hospital records might be able to give us her identity."

"She's had a lot of dental work," B.J. said. "That'll give us another resource."

Amy started past the X-ray of the pelvis, then turned back to scrutinize it more carefully. "She was pregnant." Amy unconsciously pressed her hands over her abdomen.

B.J. contemplated the film. "Jesus! The sheriff will probably see that as implicating Cam as well."

"A shame he's involved in such a mess," Dr. Epps said. "He seems like such a nice young man." While pondering the skull X-ray, he absentmindedly clicked his ballpoint pen. "No sign of head trauma." He proceeded to the chest X-ray. "Now *here's* something. This heart shadow is certainly unusual."

B.J. peered over his shoulder. "Well look at that."

"I wonder if"—Dr. Epps stepped aside so Amy could get a better view.

"What's bothering you?" she asked.

He jerked his head toward the other room. "Let's go look at the body. I noticed an odd contusion on her sternum."

Amy smiled at him. "I was hoping you would." When B.J. and Dr. Epps had arranged themselves on each side of the gurney, she continued, "I tried several types of lighting when I took my closeup shots." She pointed to slanted vertical lines of blanched epidermis two centimeters wide between four two-centimeter bands of contused flesh that ranged from four to six centimeters in length. "I wanted to make certain I captured the contrast."

B.J. cocked his head. "Doesn't look like something she'd have gotten by hitting the steering wheel."

"I'll check the car when I go to Wheeler today."

"For what purpose, Amy?" Dr. Epps took a small notebook from his jacket pocket.

"I'll put a piece of carbon paper between a couple of sheets of white paper and smack it against any object I suspect." She nodded approvingly as he scribbled down what she'd said. "We might be able to determine what object corresponds to that particular contusion."

B.J. regarded Dr. Epps with what Amy called his teacher's face. "See any defense injuries, Homer?"

Dr. Epps studied the posterior and anterior of the corpse's right arm, then switched to the left one. "Nope. Oops, wait." He picked up each hand to check for broken nails. "None, B.J."

"What's that tell you?"

"She ... uh ..." He glanced at B.J. as if looking for a hint, but B.J. pretended to be more interested in examining the woman's abdomen. "She didn't fight back, so"—a smile wreathed Dr. Epps's face—"she must have trusted her attacker."

"Your assessment would be correct," Amy said. "*If* she was murdered. However, we haven't proved that yet."

"Yes ... Oh, of course. B.J. says I must never assume anything."

B.J. winked at Amy. "How'll we know if she was dead before she went into the river?"

Dr. Epps spoke up eagerly. "I boned up on this last night. If she died from drowning, the lungs and air passages will be filled and ballooned from the additional pressure. She'll also have water in her stomach."

"Good, good, but don't forget the diatoms," B.J. said.

"Oh, yes. There will be numerous microscopic unicellular marine or freshwater algae with siliceous cell walls," Dr. Epps said as if he were reading from a text book. "Oh, and there may also be foreign matter such as sand and weeds in the lungs."

"Absolutely. If you find diatoms in the tissues, Homer, they can only have gotten there via the bloodstream. So the victim would have to have been alive when they went into the water."

"And there's a procedure to test your prognosis, Doctor," Amy said. "Dissolve a tissue sample of bone marrow or kidney in acid. If there are diatoms present, they can be seen under the microscope." She laughed. "A good botanist can even tell you whether they're from fresh water or salt water."

She stepped closer to the gurney. "While we're in a

learning mode, there's another detail I'd like you to note." She motioned to B.J. to help her turn the body over. "What do you two have to say about this?" Except for white patches on her shoulders, buttocks, and heels, the skin of the woman's back was a dark purple color.

"Aha," B.J. said. "I see what you mean. Homer, can you remember what you learned in medical school about hypostasis?"

"It's been a long time." He smoothed his hand over his thinning hair. "Something to do with gravity . . . Oh, of course, now I remember. Due to the pull of gravity, when the heart stops and circulation ceases, the blood settles in the lowest blood vessels."

"That's right," B.J. said. "For instance, if a person were to die from hanging, discoloration of the skin would appear in the lower legs and feet."

"Hmm." Dr. Epps gazed at the pattern of discoloration on the corpse. "When we found the body, it was in a sitting position. If she had died . . . well, I'll be damned"—he gestured at the body—"B.J., this is all wrong. The lividity should only be in her buttocks, feet, and legs."

B.J. clapped him on the back. "Give this man a gold star, Amy." He smiled at Dr. Epps. "Would you like to make a hypothesis as to how this pattern of hypostasis might have come about?"

"That's an easy one. She was on her back for some time." He grinned delightedly. "You reminded me that rigor mortis disappears after about thirty-six hours. So, perhaps"—he hesitated and gazed from B.J. to Amy—"Of course, I could be wrong, but perhaps her assailant waited until then to fasten her into the front seat of the car."

22

Amy parked her car beside Jed's in the lot beside Myra's Café in downtown Wheeler. The previous night, when he'd learned she'd called Ivan Fenwick and asked him to set up a meeting with Victor Samphan and Kim Sen, Jed had insisted on going to the athletic club with her.

She hurried into the restaurant and glanced around. Wicker baskets and photographs of blooming fields of tulips, lilies, and dahlias decorated the walls.

Jed hailed her from across the room and she seated herself across from him in a booth upholstered in white plastic. "Did you locate Cam?"

"None of his friends have seen him. Have you found out the time of death on our Jane Doe?"

"Not yet." She ordered toast and coffee from a waitress clad in a red pinafore and frilly white apron. "When days or weeks have elapsed, determining the time of death can be a long process. My father and Dr. Epps may make tests on body fluids, the vitreous humor of the eye, electrical responses in the muscles, and the state of digestion of the stomach contents. And after all that, the time will still not be exact."

"Great. Just what I need to hear."

"We did learn one thing. The woman was pregnant."

Jed took off his glasses and rubbed his eyes. "This whole damned case is making me crazy."

Amy took a sip of coffee. "If I get through here early enough, I'll have a friend run her fingerprints through AFIS. There might even be a missing-person bulletin out on her."

"Not with our luck, there won't be." Jed glanced at his watch. "What time's the meeting?"

"Kim at ten-thirty. Victor at eleven-thirty." She finished a piece of toast and drank the last of her coffee. "It's a three-block walk to Fenwick's; we'd better get going."

He grimaced. "I hate exercise."

"It's either that or risk having your brake line cut."

He groaned and followed her out of the restaurant. It soon became apparent that he wasn't kidding about hating exercise. She strode; he sauntered.

At last he caught hold of her hand to slow her down. "I dreamed about you last night. You should have been there." He flashed a lopsided grin. "We had one hell of a good time."

She decided to ignore his remark. His attraction to her wouldn't last long, she knew. Her midsection seemed to be growing half an inch a day; soon she'd be as big as a house.

She smiled at him and shook her head.

He twisted his face into a comical leer. "If you keep looking at me like that, I'll drag you behind a bush and have my way with you."

Amy laughed out loud. "Want to bet?" She held her coat open just far enough for him to glimpse her shoulder holster and the butt of her .38.

"My God! Do you know how to use that thing?"

"Definitely." She sobered. "I called Sheriff Boyce to tell him about the meeting."

"What'd he say?"

"That it was a stupid waste of time. Makes me wonder if he's read the autopsy reports and investigation notes I've sent him. Have you talked to Wheeler's district attorney?"

"Actually, there isn't one in residence. Chester Ingalls, the D.A. in Ursa Bay, serves a number of towns and hamlets in the county."

"Now I know how the sheriff gets away with so much." Jed chuckled. "Charley's no mental giant, that's for sure. But he's a member of one of Ursa Bay's founding families and also related to Mayor Spalding, so he doesn't have to be." He grew thoughtful as they approached the steps leading into Fenwick's Athletic Club. "You can't ask these men very many questions."

"I know. Mostly I want to watch their reactions. If neither of them is guilty, perhaps I'll learn something that'll steer us in the right direction."

At the reception desk, Daphne gave Jed an appreciative appraisal before directing them both to Ivan Fenwick's office. Fenwick and a tall, gaunt man in a dark blue suit rose to their feet as Amy preceded Jed into the room.

"Good morning, Dr. Prescott," Fenwick said with a toothy smile. He wore a sleeveless T-shirt similar to the one she'd seen him in the last time they'd met.

She shook his hand. "Mr. Fenwick, I'd like you to meet Jed MacManus, Cam Nguyen's attorney."

"Welcome to our club, Mr. MacManus." His biceps bulged as he grasped Jed's hand in an iron grip and held it until Jed glared at him and jerked his hand loose.

Fenwick observed him disdainfully before turning to the man at his side. "I asked my lawyer to sit in. Dr. Prescott, Mr. MacManus"—he gestured to the man beside him—"Elliott Osgood."

Amy and Jed shook the man's limp hand, said the proper amenities, and seated themselves on a brown tweed couch.

Fenwick buzzed the front desk, asked Daphne to page Kim, and set down the receiver. "Would anyone care for a glass of fresh carrot juice?"

"I just had breakfast," Amy said.

"Loaded with vitamin A," he said, and honed in on Jed. "Sharpens your eyesight."

"No, thanks." Jed removed his glasses and tucked them into his case.

"You interested in lifting weights, MacManus?" His gaze shifted to Amy. "Women go for hard-bodied men. Don't they Doctor?" Without giving her a chance to answer, he went on, "We're offering a mid-winter special. Since you're a friend of Dr. Prescott's, I'll even give you a discount on *that.*"

Jed thrust out his jaw. "Not interested," he said sharply.

Fenwick shrugged, smiled at Amy, and tilted back his chair.

A tap sounded on the door and Kim walked in. He smiled broadly when he saw Amy. "Ah, you are one of our little mothers." His large expressive eyes shifted to her abdomen and back to her face. "Are you in good health today?"

The elaborate pompadour his permed hair created made him appear effeminate, Amy thought.

"I'm fine," she said. "Kim, I'm Amy Prescott and this is Jed MacManus, Dr. Nguyen's attorney." When the two men had shaken hands and Kim had taken a chair, she said, "My father and I are investigating the death of Mai Nguyen. Did you know her?"

"I met her only once," he said, his face somber. "She came here with Dr. Nguyen." He wagged his head. "So sad for one so beautiful to die so young."

"Did you ever visit Dr. Nguyen at home?"

"Oh, no." Kim crossed one crisply creased trouser leg over the other and arranged his slender hands in a graceful manner. "Employees do not socialize with patrons." He smiled at Fenwick. "Boss says, you break rule, you're outta here."

"I see." Amy jotted a few words in her notebook. "How long have you lived in Wheeler?"

"Almost a year."

"Is your family here?"

"I have what you call"—he frowned—"cousins, I think."

"Dr. Nguyen had a friend named Chea Le. Did you ever meet her?"

"Chea Le," he said slowly. "I have never heard this name before."

Amy studied his fingers, thought she detected a faint yellowish stain on his index finger, and felt a chill. "What brand of cigarettes do you smoke?"

An amused smile twitched Kim's lips and he flashed his eyes at Fenwick. "Boss doesn't allow smoking."

Amy folded her arms and contemplated him in silence for a moment. "But you *are* a smoker, aren't you?"

He met her question with a bland expression. "I quit when I came to America. Your cigarettes cost too much."

Amy frowned and glanced at Jed. When he remained

silent, she said, "That's all, Kim. Thank you for meeting with us."

He beamed and dipped his head in a slight bow. "Most happy to be of assistance." He stood up and started for the door.

Amy waited until he was halfway across the room before she said, "Did you know Taun Keo?"

Kim stopped and slowly turned to face her. "Never heard this name before." He pulled his full lips into a tight line. "Will that be all, Dr. Prescott?"

"Yes, thank you."

When the door closed, she regarded Ivan Fenwick. "Did you tell him I was a doctor?"

"Let's see . . ." He rubbed his nose. "I may have, why?"

Amy shrugged. "No matter." She noted the time. "Is Mr. Samphan waiting?"

"Should be." He buzzed Daphne.

In a short time the door opened again and a man slightly taller than Amy stalked into the room. "You page me?"

"Victor, this lady would like to ask you a few questions," Fenwick said.

Amy stood up. "I'm Dr. Prescott." She paused to take in his acne-scarred skin, his rumpled hair and clothing. "But you already knew that, didn't you, Mr. Samphan?"

"You're the bi"—he halted and glanced at Fenwick—"woman who was bugging my wife." His lip curled. "I don't like people messing in my affairs."

Amy met his angry gaze straight on. "I don't like being followed, but that hasn't stopped you. Has it, Mr. Samphan?"

"Don't answer that." Elliott Osgood levered himself

out of his chair. "There'll be no accusations made here, Doctor."

Victor smirked and leaned against the wall—his fist braced on his hip, his chin in the air. "I don't know what the hell you're talking about, lady."

"What brand of cigarettes do you smoke?"

"Camels."

Amy sank down on the couch. "Did you know Mai Nguyen?"

Samphan glanced at Osgood. "Do I gotta answer *that?*" When the attorney nodded, he said, "Yeah, I knew her." He folded his arms across his chest. "Known the schitzy dame all my life."

"Schitzy?" Jed asked. "What's that supposed to mean?"

Victor jerked his head at Jed. "Who the hell is he?"

"Nguyen's lawyer," Fenwick said in a bored voice. "Answer the question and get this over with. I got a business to run."

"She always acted like she was better than everybody else."

Amy sat forward. "Why'd you call her schizophrenic?"

"She used to make up things."

"What *things* are you referring to?" Jed asked.

"In high school, she was always running to the teacher."

Jed stroked his chin as he studied the man across the room. Finally, he said, "Did she get you in trouble?"

"Mr. MacManus," Mr. Osgood said. "What are you insinuating?"

Samphan gave Osgood a dirty look. "*Sheeit,* mister, don't get your balls in a knot. I don't give a rat's ass who knows."

Osgood screwed his sharp features into a pained expression and began to clean his nails.

Samphan squinted at Jed. "Yeah, she did. So what?"

"Was that the last time the two of you had a run-in?"

"Nah, she was always making up lies about me. Told her husband I was hittin' on her."

"How long ago did this happen?"

"Four or five years ago, when they first got married."

"What did Cam do?"

"Threatened me." He sneered and flexed well-developed muscles. "I creamed him."

Amy ran her finger down a list she'd made. "Did you know Tuan Keo?"

"Who?"

"How about Chea Le?"

His eyelid twitched. "Nope."

"You ever see the Honda they pulled out of the river before?"

He licked his lips. "Not before yesterday."

"You knew Mai Nguyen's father was killed by a hit-and-run driver, right?" Amy fastened her gaze on him. "Do you know why someone would want to kill him?"

Samphan drew up his shoulders in an elaborate shrug. "The old guy acted like a fu"—he gave Fenwick a cautious glance—"like a friggin banker. Loaned everybody money. Maybe somebody didn't want to pay him back."

23

"Any gut feelings?" Amy asked as she and Jed made their way back to their cars.

"Victor Samphan's a hothead, that's for sure, and Kim is"—he made a face—"peculiar. God, I don't know. What was your impression?"

"Nothing definite. If you're not in a hurry to get back to Ursa Bay, how would you like to take a ride?"

Jed's eyes took on a wicked gleam. "Now you're talking my language."

Amy smiled and unlocked her car door. "No, I'm afraid not."

"Ah, Amy . . ." Jed slid into the seat beside her.

"Remember, you promised J.T. and J.B."

"Who?"

"The twins."

"They caught me in a weak moment." He reached across the gear shift, took her hand, and brought it to his lips. "Honey, you don't have a man and I don't have a woman." He ran the tip of his tongue along her forefinger. "What's a little sex between friends?"

"A good way to ruin a friendship, that's what." She

withdrew her hand, started the car, and pulled out into traffic.

"Where are we going?"

"To Victor Samphan's place."

"Hey now, hold it, that guy is a loose cannon. I'm not about to tangle with him."

Amy slowed the car. "Then I'd better let you out. Cause that's where I'm going."

"You are not."

Amy pulled over to the side of the road. "Jed, let's get something straight. I'm an investigator. At times, that involves taking risks. I cannot let someone tell me what I can and can't do."

"All right, all right, goddammit." Jed slashed the air with his hands. "I'm with you."

Amy smiled at him and started off once more. "I hoped you would be." She wrinkled her nose at him. "I'm not as brave as I sound."

"That's out and out coercion. It's a good thing I'm a mild-mannered person, or I might be tempted to swat you one on that cute ass of yours."

Amy laughed. "Mild-mannered! That'll be the day."

This time, although she had no difficulty finding the way, she encountered stretches where the roadbed had nearly been washed out. The station wagon pitched and bucked as she crawled through in low gear. At last, she caught sight of the river and again slowed to a crawl. She tried three byways without success.

"Tell me you're searching for a lover's lane," Jed said with a twinkle in his eyes. "And I'll forgive you for exposing me to all this"—he swept out his arm—"rusticity. I have a long list of country phobias I'm plagued by."

"Sorry." Amy glimpsed a break in the trees ahead.

"I'm looking for the place where that blue Honda might have gone into the river."

"It wasn't near the bridge?"

She shook her head. "Too many big rocks. My guess is, the current pushed the car to where the men found it."

"You think the car might not have been found if the river hadn't flooded."

"That's right." Amy stopped the car near an area of graded earth. She showed Jed where salal, fir seedlings, and wild lily-of-the-valley had been mashed down. "A vehicle went through here." She fingered the plants and inspected the ground beneath. "I wish . . ."

In squatting down beside her, Jed disturbed wild ginger leaves that scented the air. "You wish what?"

"That my friend, Nathan, was here. He could tell us exactly how long ago."

After cautioning him to walk on the untrampled side of the trail, she moved along the potholed course until the river came into full view. "The vehicle got mired in the mud."

"Looks that way." Jed regarded the shrubbery-enclosed trail they'd taken. "No one would have seen it from the road."

She proceeded with even greater care. About seventy feet from the swirling brown water, she exclaimed gleefully, "We're in luck!"

Jed crowded close. "What did you find?"

Amy broke a bracken fern, plucked off **the leaf** blades, and used the smooth, hard stalk to touch **an im**pression. "Barefooted print. Notice how the toes dig in?"

Jed leaned closer. "Yes."

"He's pushing something. And since his print overlays the car track, it must be the car." She pointed farther along where no vegetation grew. "Up there you get the full picture. A person on each side of the car."

"Both are shoving."

"On the river bank, you notice they're no longer straining."

"The car tracks go right into the river. Jesus, Amy, what do you do now?"

"Take plenty of pictures. You can help me with the video camera, and I'll mix up some dental stone to cast the foot and tire impressions."

"Why bother to put it on video?" Jed asked as they walked back to the station wagon.

"We've found it pays. If every move you make is recorded on film, no one can claim you didn't do a procedure correctly."

Amy unlocked the back of the station wagon and took out the gear she thought she'd need. As she was about to close the hatch, Jed grabbed a tarpaulin and a rolled blanket.

She observed him with a half smile. "You going camping?"

Jed pretended wide-eyed innocence. "You never know when you might need a blanket." He glanced up the road. "Where's Samphan's house?"

"Down that lane." She pointed to a sign post about thirty yards from where they stood.

Jed gave a low whistle. "You'd better get your car off the road. He might pass that way and see it."

Amy did as he suggested; she didn't want a confrontation with Victor Samphan any more than Jed did. After she'd backed down the trail as far as she dared without running the risk of getting stuck, they loaded up and trudged back to the river.

While she contorted her body into knots trying to get the camera angles she wanted, Jed meandered among gigantic cedars and Douglas fir. Sunlight worked its way through the cloud cover, heated layers of leaf mold, and white vapor threads drifted in among the tree's sweeping boughs.

"I could get to like this," Jed said as he rejoined her, no longer carrying the tarp and blanket. He moved close to where Amy was placing a ruler alongside a footprint, leaned over, and kissed her on the back of her neck. "Mmm, you and me all along in the wilderness."

Amy frowned and pointed to the video camera. "Get to work. Maybe it'll keep you out of trouble."

He gave her a suggestive look and picked up the camera. "Don't count on it."

After setting her tripod and camera aside, she fitted a metal form around the clearest tire track, took a Ziplock bag of premeasured dental stone from her supply case, and added water.

Jed watched her squeeze the plastic bag this way and that to mix the lemon-colored concoction inside. "What's that stuff."

"Calcium sulfate hemihydrate. It's a form of gypsum, the same as plaster of Paris, only dental stone produces finer detail and isn't so easily broken."

She moved uphill, opened a corner of the bag, and let the thick, creamy mixture flow slowly into the tire impression.

"Hey, what about those rocks and twigs?"

"Whatever was under the tire stays. I remove only debris that has fallen in later." She emptied the bag and started preparing the next impression.

When the casts hardened, she stored each in a separate container and carried them to the car. Jed, loaded down with her gear, trailed after her. They had just gotten the car loaded up when a blue pickup sped past.

She grabbed Jed's arm. "Duck down, it's Samphan."

"Jesus! If he finds us . . ."

She heard the spraying of gravel as the pickup skidded to a stop, then the sound of the truck backing up. "What'll we do? He knows my car."

"Improvise." Jed triggered the lock, closed the door, and grabbed her hand. "Follow me and do as I say." He dragged her into the woods. "Hurry, I've got an idea." He led the way through a tangle of shrubbery and there, spread out in a mossy glen, was the blanket.

She skidded to a stop. "Did you plan this?"

"Don't be ridiculous." He pushed her forward. "If you want to save your casts and our skin, lie down and make some appropriate noises."

A metallic thump sounded as Victor either kicked or hit her car. She dove for the blanket.

Jed flung himself on top of her. "Sorry." He tousled her hair and jerked her blouse open. "Now, kiss me."

"No. Dammit, Jed, get off of me."

This was asinine, she thought. *They should have gotten into the car, tried to bluff Samphan.* She struggled to get free. "Let me up," she whispered harshly.

When the shrubbery moved, she caught a glimpse of a green jacket and her heart thumped against her ribs. Victor Samphan could be the killer. She threw her arms around Jed's neck. "Ohh Jed . . . sweetheart." She put her lips against his ear. "He's watching."

Jed reached between them and she felt him unzip his pants. *Oh, my God.* Her cheeks blazed with embarrassment. She squeezed her eyes shut. "I'm going to die," she whispered.

Jed kissed the curve of her breast and moved his

body against hers. "If this doesn't work, we both might."

A twig snapped and Victor stepped into the clearing. Jed jerked up his head. "What the hell . . . Jesus Christ, man, can't you see we're—" He got to his feet, turned his back, and zipped his pants up. "No damned privacy anywhere."

Amy pushed herself to a sitting position, held her blouse together, and studied Victor Samphan through her tumbled hair. His eyes took in the scene skeptically and his rigid features had a pasty cast.

When he became aware of her scrutiny, his expression turned scornful. "Horny bitch!"

Blood pounded in her head and perspiration broke out underneath her clothing. *If she drew her gun, he'd attack before she could shoot. And if she did get in a lucky shot, what then? Interrupting a pair of lovers wasn't a crime.*

"Hey man," Jed said in a wheedling tone. "It's worth a hundred bucks to you if you keep this thing quiet." He held out two fifty dollar bills. "My wife will kill me if she finds out."

Samphan took a step forward, snatched the money from Jed's outstretched fingers, and stepped back. "Get your asses out of here. If you ever come here again, it'll cost you a helluva lot more than money."

Jed helped Amy to her feet. "We're going." He took up the blanket and tarp and put his arm around her.

As they edged past the man, Amy rested her hand on the gun in case he changed his mind.

"Slut!" he hissed.

She stiffened. "That's enough—" She would have lashed out at him with her fists and feet if Jed hadn't dragged her with him. "I won't let him talk to me like that."

"Oh, yes, you will." He rushed her up the trail to the car.

She got the door unlocked and snapped the keys into his hand. "You drive, I'm out of commission."

Jed didn't need any urging. He gunned the motor and tore out onto the graveled thoroughfare.

When he reached the blacktopped highway, he pulled over to the side. "Damn, I don't want to go through that again."

"Amen to that. I've never felt so—so"—she shuddered—"I need a bath."

"Jesus, Amy, he might have killed us!"

She stared at him. "Why didn't he, Jed? I'll bet money that's where that woman was murdered."

24

Amy, Dr. Epps, and B.J. gathered in the conference room for a coffee break before going their separate ways.

B.J. sipped his coffee and let out a long sigh. "Lord, what a day." He regarded Amy. "Anything interesting happen in Wheeler?"

Amy finished chewing an antacid tablet. She'd been popping them like candy all afternoon. "Not a lot. Kim Sen appears to be clean, though Victor Samphan is trouble. Evidently, some sort of conflict started between him and Mai when they were in school. He says Mai lied to Cam. That she claimed he was making passes at her when he wasn't. Cam confronted him and Samphan beat him up."

"Do you buy his story?"

"He's full of hostility, that's for sure." She pressed her hand against her churning stomach. "The place where the Honda was pushed into the river is near Samphan's home."

Dr. Epps pulled a pen and notebook from his pocket. "How do you know?"

"The route to Samphan's house runs along the river.

The area is isolated, with little or no traffic, and it's not too far from where the men found the car."

He scribbled industriously. "How did you go about verifying the location?"

The incident in the woods flashed through her mind for the hundredth time. She flushed and concentrated on peeling a strip of clear nail polish from her thumbnail. "I compared the tire imprints I took in the woods to the tires of the Honda. Same rib and cross bar configuration. And many of the other characteristics matchup." She raised her gaze to her father's. "Have you had a chance to run the license numbers I gave you through the DMV?"

"Not the ones from the cars behind Kim's rooming house. I'll try to get to it tomorrow." He levered himself out of his chair and dragged out his easel and oversized pad. "Let's see what we know about our Jane Doe."

Dr. Epps leafed through his notebook. "Female, brown eyes, black hair. Four-foot-eight-inches. Ninety-two pounds. Approximately twenty-five to thirty years old."

"I called Mrs. Waring at Harborview," Amy said. "She described Chea Le as pretty and petite with a sunny disposition. Other than that, she knew little about her. Neither did the other volunteers. What was the estimated time of death?"

"Ten to twelve days before we found her," B.J. said.

Dr. Epps turned to Amy. "I did the test you suggested on some tissue from her kidney. Guess what? No diatoms."

"Good, now we're certain she was dead before she went into the river." Amy recorded the fact in her own notebook.

"And under B.J.'s guidance, I embedded hair samples

in a block of resin and sliced cross-sections for microscopic exam." Dr. Epps pressed his hands together. "Her hair was circular, with a thick cuticle with continuous medullae." He swelled out his chest and smiled. "All characteristically Asian."

Amy grinned. "At the rate you're picking up forensics, you'll soon replace me."

His cheeks grew pink. "Never." His eyes glinted. "But it's been an exhilarating experience working with you and B.J."

"We didn't type her blood." B.J. said somewhat impatiently.

"I'll do it tomorrow and send it for a DNA," Amy said. "Was that an appendectomy scar on her abdomen?"

"Yes," B.J. said.

"How far along was her pregnancy?"

Dr. Epps regarded her with a direct gaze. "Three months."

"We'll need a DNA on the fetus too."

"Did you get one on Cam?" B.J. asked.

"Yes, but we haven't received any reports yet. Dad, was she raped?"

"No evidence of it."

"What was the cause of death?"

"Damnedest thing I've ever seen. Her chest cavity was full of blood."

"An aneurysm?"

B.J. shook his head. "We found no weakening in the wall, no evidence of ballooning, but her aorta was ruptured."

She nodded. "A fatal blow to the chest. I thought that might have been it."

Dr. Epps frowned. "Is that possible?"

"She was a tiny woman. And you saw what was done to the gardener who got in the way."

Dr. Epps continued to frown. "Did you check to see if something inside the car could have made that contusion?"

Amy emptied a large envelope onto the table. Each sheet had a labeled carbon mark. "You won't find anything there that faintly resembles the contused area."

Dr. Epps pored over the pieces of paper. "You're right, but I still can't believe anyone could rip open an aorta—"

"I know, I'd doubt it too if I hadn't witnessed a similar blow to the chest." Amy tried to keep her thoughts off Nathan. She turned to her father. "Did you measure her legs?"

"Yep. With the car seat in that position, there's no way she could have reached the brake or accelerator."

Amy blew out her breath. "It's going to be hard for Jed to sell all this to a jury." She massaged an ache in her temples. "I didn't get time to have her fingerprints run through AFIS." She stood up. "I'll go over her clothing after I eat supper. Maybe I'll find something that'll help identify her."

B.J. cleared his throat. "Did Jed meet you today?"

"Yes," she said, then stood and turned to avoid the questions about her personal life she knew he was anxious to ask. "Good night, Dr. Epps. See you in the morning, Dad," she said, excusing herself.

Upstairs, she went into her bedroom and fell across her bed. She hadn't eaten anything for lunch and she was famished, but she didn't have the energy to move.

When the ringing of the phone awakened her, the room was pitch dark. "Go away," she muttered, and rolled over. The phone continued to ring. It could be

Cam, she thought. She still didn't move. It might be Nathan. She sat up and grabbed the phone.

"Hi, babe," Jed said. "Can I come over?"

Amy flopped onto a pillow. "What for?"

"Well, I was just lying here thinking."

"Thinking about what?" Amy tried unsuccessfully to stifle her yawn.

"Dammit, you could at least pretend you're interested."

"Jed, what's the point?" she said.

"I kissed your breast today and I can't stop thinking about it."

"Jed, I like you, okay? But that's the extent of it. Please don't ever, *ever* mention this afternoon to me again. Good night." She hung up.

She got up, microwaved a TV dinner, and went down to the lab. After typing their unidentified female's blood, she went over her clothing with a magnifying glass, a laser light, and ultraviolet rays. She found nothing of interest but a wide stain on the woman's slacks and the tail of her blouse.

She moistened a corner of a clean piece of filter paper with Luminol and turned out the lights. As she touched the edge of the stain with the filter paper, the stain fluoresced, confirming her suspicion that the woman's body fluids contained blood.

She continued her experiments, but found the stain had been diluted by the long immersion in water and could tell her nothing more.

Microscopic examination of the fabric she'd found in the woman's hand showed a mixture of cotton and polymer. She debated which procedures to use. The exact shape of the torn scrap had to be preserved for comparison with the garment from which it had been torn—if they were lucky enough to find it.

That meant she couldn't do a chromatographic separation of the dye constituents. She frowned and swore. If she could show that the garment and the torn piece had the same dye composition, no one could dispute it. However, a scanning electron photomicrograph of one of the polymer fibers would suffice.

Her lab work out of the way, she dialed Hue's number. Raymond answered. After they'd greeted each other, she asked him if he knew Kim Sen.

"I've talked to him," Raymond said.

"What do you know about him?"

"Nothing. He's friendly, maybe too friendly." He laughed. "Us guys aren't sure which side of the fence he belongs on, if you get my meaning."

"Yes, I wondered if he might be gay. Do you know if he has any relatives in Wheeler?"

"I know there's another Sen in town, but I've never met him."

"What can you tell me about Victor Samphan?"

"Known him ever since we were little kids. Did you have a run-in with him?"

"Can you keep this confidential?"

"No problem."

"One of the Asian employees at Fenwick's may have had something to do with Mai's murder."

"So you're investigating Victor and Kim?"

"That's right."

"What about the janitor?"

"Mr. Fenwick didn't say anything about a janitor."

"Most of the businesses in Wheeler use Hanuman Janitorial Service."

"Spell that, please." When she finished writing the

name, she stared at it. *"Hanuman.* I've seen that name before somewhere recently."

"Probably on that old gray junker they haul their equipment in."

"That's right. It was parked behind the rooming house where Kim lives. Does he own the business?"

"I don't know, but it must be successful. The majority of the Asian businesses are clients."

Amy jotted in her notebook. "Do you know anything about an ongoing feud between Mai and Victor? This would go back to their high school days."

"I was a couple of years ahead of them in school," Raymond said. "Hue would know. She just finished putting the kids to bed and she's standing here"—he laughed and Amy heard the sound of him kissing Hue— "dying to know what beautiful lady is calling her husband." He laughed again. "Here she is."

"Hue, this is Amy."

"Amy! My husband likes to tease me."

Amy laughed.

"What can I do for you?" Hue said.

"Do you remember Mai having any trouble with Victor Samphan in high school?"

"He hassled all of us girls, especially the timid ones. One day a teacher saw Mai crying and Mai told her about Victor. The principal suspended him for a week.

"That may seem like a no big thing to some people, but to our old country parents, having a child sent home from school is a major, major disgrace. They feel it's a reflection on how they've raised their child. They probably punished Victor severely." She sighed and went on. "After he came back to school, he did some awful things to Mai."

"Like what?"

Mai sighed. "I remember that once he dumped a pile of dog shit on her books. Also, he knew Mai loved animals, so he'd search for road kills and put them in her locker. He frequently wrote nasty things about her in the boys' lavatory."

"Victor says Mai told Cam that he was making passes at her, but he claims he wasn't."

"Hah! At dances and festivals, he'd slide up to her and describe the filthy things he was going to do to her. If he'd done it to me, I'd have socked him a good one. But poor Mai was afraid of him."

"I found out he's been arrested for spousal abuse too."

"Wouldn't surprise me. Una is a lot like Mai— intelligent but shy. She even went to college. Beats me why she married Victor."

Amy thought of her own abusive marriage and cringed. "Thanks, Hue, you've been a big help."

"Was that body they found the woman you were looking for?"

"We haven't identified her yet."

"But Raymond said the car was blue and a Japanese make. I thought for sure it was the one that hit Mr. Pran."

"We found no registration papers or license plates. Not even an engine number."

"Oh, Amy. If I had your job I wouldn't sleep at night."

"That's another thing we'd better discuss, Hue. I think it would be best if you didn't tell anyone you know me. Someone could try to hurt you or Raymond because of me."

"Amy, you're the one who is most likely to get hurt. You watch out for Victor, he can be mean—real mean."

25

Amy sat hunched over the office computer, a cup of coffee perched on the small electric warmer close at hand. She'd finished typing the autopsy report and was just about to update her investigation notes when her father walked in.

"Morning, kitten," he said, bending to kiss her cheek. "What's your plan for the day?"

"I thought I'd take the fingerprints from the body and the car to the police station and check them against the criminal records. I might also stop by the courthouse in Seattle."

"If you get an address, try the reverse directory at the library."

"Good suggestion." She typed a few more words and then stopped. "I'll also check those license numbers at the Department of Motor Vehicles."

"We have anything else that's hanging fire?"

"The piece of cloth I found in the dead woman's hand is the same color blue as the Fenwick Athletic Club's uniforms. Why don't you ask Ivan Fenwick who furnishes their uniforms, and who does their laundry. If the fabrics are a match, someone's walking around in a torn uniform, or has discarded one. Find out when Wheeler's garbage is picked up and where it's dumped." She wrinkled her nose. "I sure hope we don't have to go through a ton of garbage."

"He could have buried it or burned it."

Amy smiled. "What I really hope is that it's hanging in our suspect's closet. This case needs a break like that."

"Dreamer. Did you get her blood typed?"

"Type A."

"Fine. I'll process that stain on the backseat of the car before I leave today." He came up behind her and massaged her shoulder muscles. "You've been pushing yourself too hard, kitten. Let's take some time off this evening and go out to dinner."

"Sounds great to me."

He walked off toward the laboratory door. Just before he reached it, he turned. "Why don't you ask that young lawyer fellow to come along? I haven't had a chance to talk to him."

He closed the lab door behind him before she could accuse him of setting her up. Nevertheless, she soon had Jed on the line. "My father wants to know if you'd like to go to dinner with us tonight."

"I seldom go out with women who hang up on me."

"Fine. I'll stay home and you and Dad can discuss the case."

"Do you have to be so goddamned stubborn?"

Amy let out a long breath. "Jed, I just want to be clear—I like you, we're friends, but I'm not going to go to bed with you. So do you want to go to dinner, or not?"

"Where and what time?"

"The Cove at seven."

"I'll be there. You're a cold, hard woman Amy."

"Sometimes it's easier that way."

The wealthy citizens of Ursa Bay expected their police force to do their duties efficiently but quietly. With this "out of sight, out of mind" attitude, they'd relegated their police station to the basement of the courthouse.

When Amy walked in, the reception area was quiet except for the constant ringing of phones. She set down her briefcase and asked the officer behind the counter if Sergeant Greg Hatcher was in.

"He's off today, Dr. Prescott," the desk sergeant said. "Captain Morelli is in his office if you'd like to talk to him."

"I hate to bother him. I just need someone to run some fingerprints and check on some licenses."

The sergeant leaned across the counter. *"Please* go see him," he said in a low voice. "He's in a rotten mood. He always lightens up when you come around."

Amy smiled good-naturedly. "Okay, if you say so."

She walked down a wide corridor and knocked on the captain's door.

"Come on in," a voice called gruffly.

Amy opened the door and smiled. "You sure sound cheerful today."

"Amy!" He leaped to his feet. "It's good to see you." He cleared a stack of bulletins off a chair. "Sit down. Tell me all you've been up to."

Amy laughed out loud. "You sound a bit desperate."

"You know what the Old Guard says, 'There's no crime in Ursa Bay.' Well today, it happens to be true."

"You're lucky. In the last two weeks, Wheeler has had three homicides."

"In that sleepy little burg?" He ran his hands over his graying, black curly hair, leaned back in his chair, and rested his well-shined black shoes on the desk. "Tell me all about it."

She gave him a condensed version of the investigation, but it still took thirty minutes to cover the story. "So now," she said, "I have some license numbers and fingerprints I'd like you to check for me."

"Sure thing," he said, his dark eyes alight. He got to his feet and pressed a hand to his flat stomach. "Got to do something or I'm going to get a potbelly like the cops on TV have." He chuckled and held out his hand. "Give me your prints and I'll see they're expedited."

She gave him the most recent prints plus the ones they'd gathered in the Nguyen house for comparison. After he'd allocated a man to the job, he checked the license numbers himself.

He rejoined her twenty minutes later with a computer printout. "I hope this is helpful."

"So do I." She scanned the sheet. The first two cars belonged to men who lived at the rooming house. "Hmm, this is interesting."

The captain craned his neck to see the item she was pointing to. "He's one of your suspects, isn't he?"

"Yes, Victor Samphan works at the athletic club. But I didn't know he owned the Hanuman Janitorial Service."

"Is that important?"

"I don't know." She thanked Captain Morelli and hurried out to her car.

At the North Precinct in Seattle's Public Safety Building, Amy ran into her old nemesis, Lt. Joseph

Salgado. He squinted one of his melancholy basset eyes at her. "Please tell me you're not investigating somebody in my territory."

"I'm not sure, Lieutenant. We have a Jane Doe and are hoping to get a line on her I.D. I was hoping someone might have reported her missing."

"What's her name?"

"Chea Le. A little more than two weeks ago, Dr. Cam Nguyen's wife was murdered. I'm sure you've heard about the case. The night of the murder, he says he was out with this Chea Le. But all the information we've gotten on the woman has proved to be phony. I don't have a birth date, a social security number—nothing." She shrugged and smiled. "Matter of fact, I'm not even sure that's her real name."

He laughed. "Sounds like a typical Prescott case." He motioned her to a chair. "Sit down and I'll see what I can dig up."

After awhile, he came back with a big smile. "Found her. She was arrested eight months ago for prostitution and petty larceny."

Amy glanced at the sheet of paper and saw that it included a birth date, social security number, and an address. "This is tremendous. Can you find out if she has a car registered in her name?"

A pained expression settled over his face but he trudged off. In ten minutes, he came back with another sheet of paper. "A 1992 Honda Civic. License number ATY434. Purchased at King Street Honda. The car's serial number is there too."

"Thanks for your help." She grinned at him. "I'll try not to get involved with anyone in your bailiwick."

"I'd appreciate that, Doctor. Too many fingers in the pie gives me ulcers."

Elated at the new lead, Amy drove to the address on Chea Le's arrest record. The manager of the apartments said she'd moved out months ago. She sat in her car and tried to figure out what to try next.

Her wandering gaze alighted on a café with a gray, ripped awning that flapped in the wind. A row of red metal newspaper vending machines ranged near the front door of the white stucco building.

Suddenly, an idea struck her. She stopped at the first telephone booth she came to, snatched up the yellow page directory, turned to "newspapers" and ran her finger down the list. A Cambodian newspaper! Maybe they could give her a lead.

Street lamps blinked on as she entered an area the locals called Chinatown. Lighted windows beckoned shoppers to Thai, Chinese, Japanese, and Vietnamese variety, grocery, and furniture stores. Elaborate neon signs glittered above ethnic restaurants and gave the street an exciting, exotic charm it lacked in the daylight.

Amy located the newspaper's building sandwiched between a dry cleaner and a Chinese import store. The room she entered was lighted by a single globe in the ceiling. Shelves that held pencils, scratch pads, reams of paper, boxes of envelopes, and rolls of adding machine tape ranged in tiers on age-darkened walls. In a shadowy corner, a covered printing press crouched like a black, humpbacked beast.

An Asian woman with thin gray hair and a multitude of wrinkles sat on a stool at a long table rolling newspapers and sliding them into clear plastic sleeves. "You needing something?" she asked in a reedy voice.

"I'm looking for a young woman named Chea Le."

The woman blinked and knotted her fingers together

in front of her. "I fine out." She pattered across the room and through a door.

Amy heard a clamor of voices speaking in a language she didn't understand. The next moment, a group of people poured out of the door—two men, one who looked to be in his thirties and one in his mid-fifties; two women of about the same ages; and a couple of little girls.

At the sight of her, all the adults stopped and again had a spirited consultation. One of the little girls clung to the younger woman's leg. The other one edged around her mother and sucked her finger as she fixed Amy with an unblinking stare.

The wrangling ceased and the younger man was pushed forward. "I am Antoan Yong," he said. "My family want to know who you are."

"Dr. Amy Prescott," she said, holding out her I.D. All of them crowded around to see it. "I'm an investigator. I'm looking for a woman named Chea Le."

She made eye contact with each of the adults. "Did any of you know her?" As soon as the words were out of her mouth, she realized she'd used the past tense and cursed her stupidity.

Silence fell as each of them weighed her. "I know Chea," the young woman said. "We were in school together. My mother-in-law"—she gestured to the older woman—"and her mother were friends before Chea's mother died."

"Does she live in this neighborhood?"

The young woman and Antoan exchanged glances and Amy wondered if they knew about the prostitution charge.

"She comes and goes," the young woman said.

Antoan's mother asked him a question and he relayed it to Amy. "Why are you looking for Chea?"

"I work for a lawyer. He is defending a man who has been accused of murdering his wife. This man says he was with Chea the night his wife was killed. So the lawyer wants to talk to Chea to find out if the man is telling the truth."

The young man translated, the others said, "Ahh," nodded their heads, and another heated exchange took place. Finally, the older man spoke sharply and gestured to his son.

"Chea works as a hostess at the Golden Turtle Lounge."

Amy checked the time and found it was five o'clock. "How do I get there?"

The older woman scowled and started shouting at her husband and son. Antoan threw up his hands. "My mother says you should not go there alone." With solemn expressions, the rest of the group nodded in agreement.

"Why not?"

"Bad place," the mother said emphatically. "Very bad."

26

Amy steered her car into traffic, then turned to Antoan. "Why does your mother think the Golden Turtle is a bad place?"

"My parents are old-country people." Antoan regarded her for a moment. "Have you heard about Pol Pot and his Khmer Rouge?"

"Yes."

"The terrible times my parents went through made them paranoid." He uttered an embarrassed laugh. "They're always imagining they see Polpotites. Turn right at the next light."

"From what I hear, Mr. Yong, they may be right."

He stared at her, the streetlights glinting on the whites of his eyes. "You're joking."

"No, I'm not." Amy signaled and turned onto a darker, narrower street. "The FBI think former members of the Khmer Rouge have infiltrated many of the Asian communities."

"No"—he firmed his lips and shook his head—"Immigration is very strict. They'd never allow such a thing to happen."

"Aliens have been coming ashore here, or sneaking

over Canada's border, for years. There are probably many more illegals here than we think."

"No way, Dr. Prescott. Everyone in the neighborhood would be talking about it. There"—Antoan pointed to a two-story, tile-roofed building with sweeping up-tilted eves—"that's the Golden Turtle." A sign with hundreds of glistening gold lights outlined the image of a turtle. "Park at the side," Antoan said.

Amy did as he instructed and turned off the ignition. "Does your mother think the Golden Turtle is connected to the Khmer Rouge?"

"She says Mr. Chinn, the owner, collaborated with them." Antoan made a face. "She has not yet learned to trust people."

Amy took in a breath and let it out slowly. "I hope she's wrong." She checked her shoulder holster. "Thank you for showing me the way."

"I'd better come in with you."

Red lacquered panels trimmed with intricate gold and black scrolls framed the dimly lighted foyer. Massive bronze Fu-Lion dogs crouched on either side of the entryway. A massive Asian, wearing a blue suit that threatened to part at the seams if he flexed a muscle, leaned against the archway leading into the lounge.

He regarded her imperiously as she approached. "Tourists aren't welcome here," he said.

"I'm Dr. Amy Prescott. I'd like to see Mr. Chinn."

"Make an appointment."

"No"—she narrowed her eyes—"I'll call Police Lt. Salgado instead." She hoped the lieutenant never found out how often she used his name. "He sent me to see Mr. Chinn. He's not going to like it when he finds out I was prevented from speaking with him."

"What you want?"

"I'd rather discuss my business with Mr. Chinn."

He pointed a sausage-sized finger at her. "Wait here." He marched across a darkened room filled with small tables. On each one, stubby candles flickered in gold-colored glass containers.

Amy moved inside the archway to get her eyes accustomed to the darkness. A bar lined with stools occupied one wall. On the other side of the room, tables bordered a small dance floor. A couple danced to a Dinah Washington tune that was playing on the juke box.

The doorman came back and growled, "He'll give you five minutes." He jerked his bullet-like head and started back the way he'd come.

Amy and Antoan followed him down a corridor decorated with gold foil wallpaper printed with soft charcoal renderings of bamboo. A number of doors opened off the corridor and at the far end, a stairway led to the second floor. From behind one of the doors came the voices of a number of men.

Their escort knocked at the door closest to the stairs. When a man said, "Come," their escort let them in and left.

A man dressed in a pale pink shirt and black suit sat behind a teakwood desk. He had broad cheekbones, a long face, and a square chin. He wore a diamond ring on his right hand and his open-throated shirt displayed a heavy gold chain around his neck.

In a nearby corner stood a mirror-lined and glass-fronted curio cabinet filled with Shoushan stone chops depicting the Chinese astrological years. Off to the man's right, a sliding glass door led to an enclosed bonsai garden with hidden lighting.

She and Antoan crossed the room, their feet sinking

into plush silver gray carpet. Mr. Chinn got to his feet. Amy was surprised to find he was over six foot tall.

"I am Mr. Chinn, Dr. Prescott," he said, letting his gaze travel over her. "This is a delightful surprise." His smooth vanilla voice sent a riffle of apprehension along her skin. "I must say, doctors have certainly changed since I last saw one." He turned up the corners of his mouth in a smile that didn't reach his eyes.

She put out her hand. "Thank you for seeing me, Mr. Chinn." She gestured to Mr. Yong who had halted several steps behind her. "Do you know Antoan Yong?"

"We've met." Mr. Chinn's attention didn't shift to Antoan, nor did he offer to shake hands. "What can I do for you, Doctor?" he said, waving them toward a couple of straight-backed chairs in front of his desk.

"I'm an investigator, Mr. Chinn. Mr. Yong tells me a young lady by the name of Chea Le works here."

Mr. Chinn swiveled his head slowly and his black eyes honed in on Mr. Yong like a timber rattler on a ground squirrel.

Mr. Yong twisted his fingers together. "I—I may have been mistaken, of course."

Mr. Chinn lifted one shoulder dismissively and once more focused on Amy. "Why are you looking for this woman?" he asked.

Amy repeated the story she'd told the Yong family and added, "Does she still work here?"

"No. I can't depend on her. Comes in late, doesn't show up when she's supposed to."

"When did you last see her?"

He picked up a needle-sharp letter opener with a green jade handle. Without taking his eyes off of her, he tilted back in his white leather chair and cleaned his fingernails while he pondered her question.

In the silence, sounds from the adjoining rooms became more apparent to her. The murmur of men's voices seeped in from one side. From overhead came a woman's laughter, then a rhythmic thumping sound. As she realized the probable cause of the noise, her cheeks flamed.

Mr. Chinn observed her embarrassment with a half smile and raised one eyebrow a fraction. The sounds escalated and Mr. Yong squirmed with discomfort.

"My sister." Mr. Chinn pointed his chin toward the ceiling. His eyes met Amy's. "Quite insatiable." He took a black record book from a drawer and ran the letter opener's glistening tip down the page. "The last time Chea Le graced us with her presence was January the twelfth."

"Do you have an address, or a phone number where I might reach her?"

"I don't keep employee records." He stood up. "If there's nothing further, I have work to do." Amy and Mr. Yong rose to their feet and started for the door.

"Yong," Mr. Chinn said. "A word, please."

When Amy stepped into the corridor, she pulled the door to her until it almost closed and stood with her back to it.

"Don't you ever interfere in my business again," Mr. Chinn said in a cold, hard tone, keeping his voice low. "Otherwise, you and your family won't have a business, nor a building to run it in. Clear?"

"Yes, Mr. Chinn. So sorry, Mr. Chinn. It'll never happen again, Mr. Chinn."

Amy hurried down the corridor, edged into the lounge, and sat down at a table. When a cocktail waitress approached her, Amy ordered an orange seltzer and asked, "Do you know where I can find Chea?"

The woman looked at her with a startled expression. "Why?"

"A man might go to prison if I don't find her." Much to her exasperation, Antoan picked that moment to appear in the doorway. With a scared look, the waitress backed away and returned to the bar. Amy swore under her breath as she watched Antoan scurry across the room without looking right or left.

Amy scanned the faces of the happy hour crowd. At a nearby table, two men sat talking, their faces intent. One turned his head and she glimpsed a scar that extended from his cheekbone to his ear.

She frowned and chewed the edge of her lip. Not too long ago, she'd seen a scar like that, but she couldn't remember where. She started as the waitress appeared at her side. She set down the seltzer, gave Amy her change, and left.

When Amy lifted the bottle, she found a small, folded piece of paper. She palmed it, got up, and went to the rest room. Once inside the stall, she unfolded the note and found a message that read, *Meet me in the parking lot in fifteen minutes.*

Amy sauntered back to her table, sipped her drink, making it last as the minutes dragged by. Finally, she rose and made her way to the parking lot. At the back of the building, nearly obscuring the rear exit door, stood a large green dumpster. Amy waited in the shadows.

Five minutes. Ten. Twenty. Amy had begun to lose hope when the exit door opened and the woman slipped through. "Over here," Amy whispered.

The woman ran to her. "We can't talk here."

"I have a car."

"Good." She crouched down beside the dumpster. "Start the motor, open the back door, and I'll get in."

Mission accomplished, Amy took off down the street with the waitress crouched on the floor behind the front seat.

"Sorry." the woman said. "I don't dare let anyone see me talking to you."

"Why not?"

"The whole place was on full alert the instant you went into Chinn's office."

"Because of the gambling rooms and the prostitution upstairs?"

"How did you know?"

"I'm an investigator. I worked at the crime lab in Seattle at a time when there were several stabbings in this area. I learned the nature of the business conducted in a place like that."

She turned onto a quiet residential street, pulled over, and shut off the motor. "What's your name?"

The woman was perched on the edge of the backseat, wringing her hands. "Lian Choy."

"What can you tell me about Chea Le?"

"We rent an apartment together."

"Is she home? Can I talk to her?"

Lian shook her head agitatedly. "She's not there. I haven't seen her in two weeks." A sob tore from her throat. "I didn't know what to do. She wouldn't like it if I talked to the police."

"Because she's involved in prostitution?"

"That was Chinn's doing."

Amy stared at her. "What do you mean?"

"If Chinn asks a girl to come work in his crib and she won't, he has a friend of his on the police force pick her up on a prostitution charge."

"Oh, now I see. Mr. Chinn pays her bail, she comes to work, and never gets out of debt."

"You got it. The dirty, rotten bastard."

"Was Chea dating anyone?"

"Yes, but I never met him. We worked different shifts."

"Did she leave anything in the apartment that'd give me an idea of where she might have gone, or who she might have been seeing?"

Lian shook her head. "One day I got home from work and everything except her furniture was gone. All her clothing. Even her books."

"Did she leave a note?"

"Nothing." She drew in a tremulous breath. "We've been friends for a long time. It's not like Chea to walk out on people."

"Did any of the neighbors see her move out?"

"The woman down the hall said she saw a man she didn't know in the hall."

"Does she remember anything about him?"

"I was so upset, I didn't ask her."

"Did Chea have a car?"

"Uh-huh. She borrowed from Chinn to get it. Said she might as well, she'd be working on her back for the rest of her life anyway."

Amy turned, knelt on the front seat and took the other woman's hands. "What kind of a car?"

Lian saw the look on her face and tears overflowed her eyes. "Oh, God, something awful has happened to her, hasn't it?"

"What's the color and make?"

"A-a . . ." Her slender body shook. Her teeth chattered. Finally, she got the words out. "A b-blue Honda."

27

Amy arrived at the Cove Restaurant ten minutes late and headed for the rest room. She combed her wind-blown hair and put on some lipstick. In her haste, she moved too quickly. She winced as the nagging pain in her back radiated into her side.

She pressed her hand against the sore spot and sank onto a padded stool. God, she was tired. The thought of dealing with Jed and her father at once added to her weariness.

With a resigned sigh, she rose and went to find their table.

Both men stood up as she approached. B.J. put his hand on her shoulder. "Have a bad day?"

"You could say that." She seated herself.

Jed gave her a long, cool look, sat down, and picked up his drink. "So, do we know who the dead woman is?"

"Captain Morelli said he'd put a rush on the finger-prints." She took her notebook from her purse. "Victor Samphan owns the gray van I saw behind Kim's place."

"The one that had Hanuman Janitorial Service painted on it?" B.J. asked.

She nodded, saw the waiter advancing on them, and scanned the menu.

After the waiter had taken their order, B.J. said, "So Victor and Kim may be in this together."

"Not necessarily. Victor could have been doing some cleaning." She glanced at the next item in her book. "Chea Le has an arrest record for prostitution and petty larceny in Seattle."

Jed rattled the ice in his empty glass. "Did you get an address?" He signaled the waiter and pointed to his glass.

"She no longer lives there. I talked to a woman who has been sharing an apartment with Chea."

B.J. beamed at her. "Good work, kitten."

She paused as the waiter served their salads. "Chea moved out two weeks ago and her friend hasn't heard from her since."

"The timing's right." Jed took a long pull on the drink a cocktail waitress had delivered, picked up his fork, and attacked his salad. "B.J. says the woman died at least ten to twelve days ago."

"True," Amy said. "According to Chea's friend, she bought a blue Honda not too long ago. I've got a license number of ATY434; I also have a serial number."

"Didn't our witness to the hit-and-run say the license number contained an A and a 4?" B.J. asked.

"That's right."

"But he also said a man was driving." B.J. tugged the edge of his mustache. "So someone in Wheeler had access to her car."

"Looks that way." Amy switched her attention to Jed. "Did my father tell you the tire tracks I cast match those of the Honda?"

"Yes."

She made a small check mark on her list. "Dad, I don't think I mentioned that it appeared as if the vehicle might have gotten mired in the mud."

"Aha! The killer may have been forced to leave the body in the car until he and his accomplice could get the vehicle out." He nodded and stroked his beard. "He killed her and left her lying on the rear seat."

"What did the stain show?" Amy said as she scribbled down the information.

"Body fluids soaked through to the padding. Type A blood. I sent out for a PCR."

She shifted on her chair, but a change of position didn't ease the ache in her back. She gave up and nibbled a piece of cucumber. "Anything else new?"

"A DNA report came in. Mai was raped by two men."

"Oh, God." She gripped the edge of the table. "Cam wasn't one of them, was he?" She waited impatiently while the waiter served their dinner.

"No," B.J. said with a kindly expression. "The DNA of saliva taken from the cigarette butts we found in the woods were from the same two men. And the tissue from under her fingernails matched one of them." He made a face. "Now all we need is a couple of suspects."

"Have either of you seen an Asian man with a scar on the right side of his face?"

B.J. paused with his fork halfway to his mouth. "What about him?"

"I saw him in a cocktail lounge in Chinatown." She frowned and searched her memory again. "I'm almost certain I've seen him before."

"So you spent the day in a cocktail lounge." Jed emptied his glass and signaled for a refill. "No wonder you're so tired."

Amy caught his eye and raised an eyebrow, meaningfully. "Did you hear from Cam?" she asked, hoping to keep his attention on the case.

"Me hear from a man who expects me to save him

from death row? Don't be ridiculous. I'm obviously pretty marginal to this entire case."

"That's not true, Jed."

"It isn't? Would you care to give me your interpretation, *Doctor?*"

B.J. lay his napkin beside his plate and got to his feet. "You'll have to excuse me, kids, I've got some work to finish."

Amy turned to him with an angry expression. "Dad!"

"See you in the morning, Amy."

Amy clenched her teeth. There ought to be a law against fathers who played cupid.

Jed leaned across the table. "What do you think I am? A dirty old man? You don't have to bring your father along to keep me from touching you."

Amy set down her fork. "This isn't working out, Jed. Perhaps it would be better if you contacted another investigator."

"I don't want anyone else, dammit. I want you."

"No, you don't. You're rebounding from a divorce and you're trying to fill the void."

"I just want to hold you."

She shook her head. "That isn't enough for you and you know it." She massaged her throbbing forehead. "I'm going through a pretty traumatic time myself. I don't have the strength to cope with your emotional needs as well as my own."

"Am I that hard to take?"

"No, of course not. You're an attractive man. I'm sure a dozen women in this room would be glad to go home with you."

"Then why won't you?"

"I told you why this morning." She tossed her napkin on the table and stood up. "Evidently we can't keep this relationship on a professional basis. I think you'd better get someone else."

"I'm sorry." He gazed at her with a stricken expression. "Please stay, Amy. I've had a bit too much to drink, I guess. I promise I'll stick to business."

Damn! she thought. She sank back onto the chair. When she got home, her father was going to get an earful.

Amy gathered an arm load of towels from the top of the drier, trudged into the bedroom, and began to fold them. The previous night had been a replay of countless evenings she'd spent with her ex-husband. She'd sat in the lounge at the Cove until twelve o'clock, listening to Jed's tearful story of his failed marriage. Then she'd taken him home because he was too drunk to drive.

She stowed the towels in the linen closet, got dressed, and tried to quiet her quivering nerves. Today, she'd be interviewing the two women who'd answered her newspaper ad for a nanny.

The first one she'd arranged to meet at ten. The second one's appointment was this afternoon.

Upon realizing a live-in nanny might be as abrasive as a bad marriage, she'd given the interviews a lot of thought. She'd decided to try a two-part system. First, they'd meet in a neutral setting just to talk so she could get an impression of whether or not the woman fit her qualifications. If the applicant passed the initial test, she would arrange a second meeting at the apartment for an in-depth conference to decide if she and the woman were compatible.

On her way out, Amy stopped in the office to talk to her father. She found him at the computer. "Were you able to learn anything about the piece of cloth?"

"The athletic club does its own laundry. They send garments to a seamstress in Wheeler if they need mending."

"Great. Did you talk to her?"

"I tried, but the lady and I had a language barrier. She was also obviously terrified."

"Then she's not any more likely to talk than the man who witnessed the hit-and-run."

"What about asking your friend Hue to speak to her? The woman might tell her things she wouldn't tell us."

"It's worth a try. Anything else?"

B.J. grinned. "After I made a few threats, Fenwick dug up a worn shirt for fabric comparison." He rubbed his hands together. "Matched our scrap exactly, right down to the polymer fibers."

"Fantastic." She leaned against the edge of the desk and swung her leg. "I'd like to discuss last night."

"Nice fellow, that Jed. Good personality. Sharp mind. He'll go places." He shot a quick glance in her direction. "Did you and he clear up your differences?"

"Jed's stubborn, opinionated, sexist, and he's got a quick temper."

"Ah . . . you have similar personalities. That's a start."

She folded her arms. "He's just gone through a divorce and he drinks too much. I had to drive him home and put him to bed."

"He'll straighten up. Any man might react that way under the same circumstances."

"Oh, really? After he 'straightens up' will he stop trying to get me into bed?"

B.J.'s ears turned red. "Most men get around to that sooner or later, don't they?"

"Oh, they do, do they?" She slid off the desk and braced her hands on her hips. "How dare you condemn me for having Nathan's twins, yet say it's all right for me to sleep with Jed."

"I didn't mean it that way."

"Yes you did and don't you ever pull a stunt like last night again."

"But ... dammit, Amy, I only want to—"

"I know what your intentions are. Do I keep lining up middle-aged matrons for *you* to date?"

"I'm used to being alone." He thrust out his chin. "I don't need anyone."

"That is a lie. You've never been alone. You've always had me either at home or only a phone call away. If I left town, you'd be beating the bushes for a woman who'd move in with you."

"See? You admit it yourself. Everybody needs a partner. Someone to share their joys and triumphs with." He regarded her with a crestfallen expression. "That's all I want for you."

"Okay, but what about what *I* want, Dad? Shouldn't that be at least as important?" When he only regarded her sadly, she turned and walked out of the office.

Tongue-and-groove pine and booths upholstered in brown calico gave the Maple Leaf Café a cozy atmosphere. Amy located Madge Zimmer and took a seat across from her. "Thank you for coming, Ms. Zimmer," she said, and smiled warmly at the woman.

"I expected to be invited to your home." Madge Zimmer tossed her head and not a hair dislodged from the woman's lacquered blond coif. Her gaze traveled over Amy's woolen hunter-green slack suit. "I couldn't help wondering if there was something you didn't want me to know."

"Not at all," Amy said with forced cordiality. "I decided

a less formal approach would be better for the initial meeting." She beckoned to a waitress. "Shall we have brunch?"

Amy ordered tea and a chicken salad. When Ms. Zimmer hesitated over the menu, Amy said. "Order anything you like, I'm paying."

The woman chose sliced roast sirloin of beef with a wine glaze and chocolate cake for dessert.

"Are you married?" Amy asked as they started on their salads.

"Not anymore." Ms. Zimmer pulled her lips into a tight line. "And good riddance. No sense of responsibility. Took off the minute the children got out of high school. Left me with nothing but a house and a beat-up car."

"Well, you still have your children." Amy poured cream into her tea.

A drop of cream landed on the tabletop and Ms. Zimmer wiped it up before it even had a chance to settle. "Humph," she said. "They're scattered to the wind. Never write. Don't give a whit whether I'm alive or dead."

A chunk of chicken stuck in Amy's throat and she gulped water to get it down. "That's too bad. Maybe they'll visit when they have families." She pulled a ceramic container toward her and extracted some sugar substitute. Before she had the corner torn off the packet, Ms. Zimmer had restored both the sugar and cream to its proper place.

Ms. Zimmer finished her salad and started on the entrée. "My daughter has a boy three and a girl two."

"That's nice. I'll bet you enjoy them."

"I might if she'd discipline them once in a while." Ms. Zimmer used her knife to separate baby carrots from asparagus tips and the asparagus tips from her sliced sirloin. "They run through the house whooping and yelling like a bunch of Indians."

Amy set down her teacup and laid her crumpled napkin on the table. "Thank you for your time, Ms. Zimmer. I believe I've learned all I need to know." She stood up. "I'll get the check."

On the way home, a feeling of hopelessness came over her. If Madge Zimmer was the type of woman who thought herself qualified to care for children, she'd never find the right person.

When she arrived at the office, her father was gone and the red light on the answering machine was blinking.

She pushed the button and her heartbeat quickened at the sound of Nathan's voice. "Amy," he said, his deep mellow voice drawing out the syllables in a way she'd grown accustomed to. "You're in danger. Call me tonight at eight."

After replaying the tape three times just for the pleasure of hearing Nathan's voice, she erased it and sat down at the computer to finish typing her case progress notes.

She had scarcely gotten started when the phone rang. Annoyed at the interruption, she snatched up the receiver and said curtly, "Prescott and Prescott, forensic investigators."

"Amy, this is Captain Morelli. I've got the results on those fingerprints you brought in."

"Your department is super efficient, Captain."

"We aim to please," he said and laughed. "The prints found on the seat adjustment lever and the Honda's steering wheel are the same as your suspect number one. Those taken from the sides and trunk of the car match those of suspect number one and suspect number two. So your two perps were also involved in the second woman's death. However, AFIS still doesn't have a thing on either one of them."

"How about our Jane Doe?"

"Oh yes, let's see . . ." Amy heard the sound of shuffling papers. "Here it is. No wonder I didn't remember the name, it's an odd one. Your Jane Doe is a Miss Chea Le."

28

Amy sat at a corner table in a deli on the fringe of the Thaxton University campus, watching students rush in and out. She studied each girl, wondering if she could be the person the university counselor had called her about as a possible nanny for the twins.

She focused on a young woman standing just inside the front door, her shoulders hunched, her eyes downcast. Amy recognized the stance. God knows it'd taken her long enough to break herself of that self-conscious posture.

Her attention shifted to an impromptu touch-football game going on outside the window. Rain clouds had given way to sunshine. The fair weather seemed to have put everyone in high spirits.

A tremulous voice broke her out of her reverie. "Dr. Prescott?"

Amy looked up to find the woman she'd been watching moments before hovering near her table. The tall, thin woman's straight black hair hung to the middle of her back and she looked to be older than the other students Amy had seen.

Amy smiled at her. "Yes, I'm Dr. Prescott."

The young woman twisted her hands together. "I'm Mary Little Bear. My counselor said to meet you here."

"Thank you for coming, Mary," Amy said. "Would you like to talk here, or shall we walk?"

Mary brushed her hair out of her eyes and peered around at the young people sprawled on wooden chairs, all eating and talking at the same time. "It gets pretty noisy in here."

Amy got to her feet. "Okay, let's walk. I haven't had my exercise for the day." She regretted the decision when she discovered that Mary was a fast walker. "Let's sit a bit," Amy said when she spotted a bench. "I'm afraid I'm out of shape." She grinned at Mary. "In more ways than one."

"How far along are you?" Mary asked hesitantly.

"Only four months, but I'm expecting twins."

"Twins." Mary settled down on the bench beside her. "That's nice. Is—is this your first pregnancy?"

Amy nodded. "Do you have brothers and sisters?"

Mary picked at a ragged cuticle. "I'm the oldest of seven."

"Wow, that must be a handful."

"Sometimes." Mary relaxed against the back of the wooden bench. "But I'm used to it." She folded her hands in her lap and gazed across the campus.

After several moments of silence, Amy realized she'd have to initiate the discussion. "Why don't you tell me something about your childhood?"

Mary looked startled. "Like what?"

"Oh, I don't know," Amy said, waving her arms. "What you did. What your mother is like." She spread her hands. "Just talk, so I can get to know you. I'm new at this sort of thing."

"I'm not too good at talking," Mary said, her eyes

flashing with self-deprecating humor. "The kids at school used to call me long, tall, tight-lipped Mary."

"I used to get skinny ninny all the time." Amy chuckled. "I can laugh about it now, but it sure wasn't funny then. I never seemed to fit in."

Mary's lips parted in a lopsided smile. "Neither did I." She pushed restless hands into the pockets of her jacket. "My father died when I was five and my mother remarried. I was six when she had the first baby and every few years she'd have another one. If my stepfather couldn't find a job, my mother would go to work and I'd take care of the house and kids."

"How old is the youngest?"

"Six." A gentle smile lifted the corners of her mouth. "I helped deliver Jacy." She smiled again. "I think he was the prettiest of all of them."

"You were there when she delivered?"

"I tried to be. Whenever she got close to her time, I'd beg her not to have the baby until I got home from school. If I was there, the midwife would let me help with the delivery." She interlaced fingers whose nails had been bitten to the quick and let out a long sigh. "I sure miss them." She swallowed and blinked her eyes.

"I can see how you would. I was an only child and I used to long for a sister. But my mother deserted us and my father never remarried." She chewed the inside of her bottom lip. *He should have,* she thought. He had too much love and not enough people to give it to.

She blew out her breath and glanced at Mary. "I suppose you put off college because of the children."

"That's right. I'm nearly twenty-seven and my mother kept worrying that I was waiting too long, but I didn't want to leave until Jacy started school."

Her face lit up. "The first day, he was so proud. He

put on his new clothes and marched out to wait for the
school bus with the rest of the kids. Funny little guy
kept setting his shiny red Mickey Mouse lunch box on
the ground and opening it up. She laughed. "He's some
kid."

"Where do they live?"

"Kamiah, Idaho."

Amy tried to remember the Idaho map she'd studied
so closely the previous fall. "Where is that?"

"Up in the shank of the Idaho boot. Just inside the
Nez Perce Reservation. The closest town of any size is
Orofino."

Orofino! Nathan was born and raised there. Amy
gripped her purse in both hands. Surely this had to be a
sign. "Do you speak the Nez Perce language?"

Mary stiffened and swung to her feet. "Why do you
want to know?"

Amy met her defensive stare. "My twins are half Nez
Perce. I want them to learn their father's language and
culture."

"What could I teach them that he can't?"

Amy's lip started to tremble. She took a deep breath.
"They won't ever see him. We aren't married."

"Oh . . . The counselor didn't tell me that you—"

"Does the fact that I'm not married bother you?"

"No . . . it . . . uh, just kind of surprised me. You being a doctor and all." She bent her head and stared at
her scuffed loafers. "Back home people say such things
only happen to us stupid Indians."

"People with small minds have to find some way to
make themselves feel superior. You didn't say whether
or not you spoke the language."

"Yes." She smiled shyly. "And I know the songs, the
stories, and the dances."

"That's wonderful." Amy beamed at her. "Would you be interested in living with me and taking care of the twins?"

"Are you close to the college? I don't have a car."

"We may have to get you a bicycle. The apartment is on Endicott Street."

Mary laughed. "I can walk that easy. When will you want me?"

"As soon as you can move in. I want to have a natural birth if I can, and I'll need a labor coach. Are you working somewhere?"

"I wash dishes from six to twelve out at Logger's Roost."

"Jeez, Mary, that's a tavern—and a rough one at that. How do you get there?"

"I walk."

"In the rain? My God, it's at least five miles each way. And there aren't any streetlights."

"I'm a fast runner."

Amy shook her head. "It's a dangerous part of town. Working for me, you won't need that job. Quit, okay?"

"I'd have to give them a few days' notice."

"Okay, if you must." Amy raked her fingers through her hair. "But at least let me take you to work and pick you up when you get through."

"I'll be all right, Dr. Prescott. I've been walking in the dark all my life."

"Maybe so," Amy said, scowling at her. "But a woman is unsafe on the streets at night, alone and unprotected." She grasped the young woman by the shoulders. "You be careful. I've seen some terrible things."

29

Amy parked her car in the private parking area behind their building. Here, they had taken a number of precautions. Photocell sensors turned on a sodium floodlight at dusk. A deadbolt secured the door that opened onto a short corridor; the door leading upstairs also had a deadbolt.

She accepted the system as a necessary measure to protect them and the evidence on which they worked. Now, viewing it from Mary Little Bear's point of view, she wondered if the young woman might not feel as if she were imprisoned.

She hurried past several doors and worked the lab's combination lock. Her father would probably be inside, and she was anxious to share the news she'd gotten at the doctor's office with him.

In the brightly lit autopsy room, B.J. stood at a counter putting away the sterilized knives, forceps, chisels, and electric saw blades he and Dr. Epps had used while performing Chea Le's autopsy.

"Hi," he said. "You look excited. What's up?"

She regarded him with a rather belligerent set to her chin. If he didn't react as a grandfather should this time, she wouldn't share anything else regarding her pregnancy with him. "I had an ultrasound today."

"Everything all right?"

"Yes. The doctor says the twins are boys."

"That's grand, kitten. Just grand." He gave her a hug. "Have you decided what you're going to call them?"

She noticed the forced joviality in his voice, but she smiled and patted his arm anyway. Neither one of them functioned very well when they were at odds with each other.

"How do you like the sound of Joshua Berkley, after you?" B.J. grimaced as she knew he would. "And Jeremy Tate, after Nathan's father?"

"Joshua's getting the worst of the deal. I hope he can tolerate Berkley better than I did." He lay an electric motor on a shelf beside a mallet and a rongeur. "A woman by the name of Lian Choy called and left her number. It's in the office."

"Good. I suggested she talk to the people in her apartment complex to find out if any of them saw Chea Le the day she moved." Amy headed for the office.

When she dialed Lian's number, the woman answered so promptly Amy wondered if she'd been waiting right beside the phone. "This is Dr. Amy Prescott," Amy said. "Did you learn anything about Chea Le?"

"A little. Our manager assigns renters a specific parking space. The man who lives directly in front of Chea's saw her leave two weeks ago. That's the last time he saw her car."

"Was her car packed, do you know?"

"No."

"What was she wearing?"

Lian's voice faltered and Amy heard her blow her

nose. "A red b-blouse with a dark gray blazer and slacks."

Amy caught her breath. The same clothing she had on when she was killed. "What about the man someone observed on your floor?"

"That woman says she saw him twice. He carried out several large garbage bags and dumped them in a blue pickup."

Victor Samphan? "Could she describe him?"

"He was Asian and had a scar on his face."

Could there be a connection between him and Samphan? Amy's pulse began to race. "I saw him in the lounge the night I talked to you."

"Yes, he comes in about once a week, but he couldn't have had anything to do with Chea leaving."

"Why not?"

"She hated him. Chinn made her go upstairs with him. The man beat her when she resisted him. She would never have gone anywhere with him."

"Lian, you realize you mustn't discuss this with anyone, don't you?"

"I guess so. But she—she's g-gone."

Liam sobbed brokenly and Amy felt her own eyes growing watery. "What'll I do, Dr. Prescott?"

"Don't do anything. Chea's fingerprints have been identified, so we're positive it's her. The news of her death will be showing up in the papers soon."

"What about the man with the scar?"

"Don't mention him. Not to anyone, Lian. You understand? These men have killed four times. They won't hesitate to kill again."

B.J. came through the lab door as Amy hung up. "What did she say?"

"Chea left two weeks ago wearing the same clothes

she had on when she went into the river. A man with a scar on his face was seen putting some garbage bags into a blue pickup."

"Got any idea how this man with the scar fits into this?"

She shook her head. "I have a vague feeling I've seen him before somewhere in Wheeler."

"Maybe"—he ran his hand over his beard and stared into space—"we could talk Sheriff Boyce into bringing in Victor Samphan for questioning?"

"He might . . . for you. Want to try?"

He grinned. "Let's drive over there tomorrow and give it a shot. All he can do is say no."

"Good idea. I'll go to my exercise class while you're at the jail. I want to speak to Hue." Amy lay her notebook beside the computer. "I'll assemble our facts so the sheriff can't say we're just trying to get Cam off the hook."

B.J. leaned down and kissed her on the cheek. "See you in the morning about nine. Don't work too long."

Amy stayed at the computer until seven. The report had taken much longer than it should have because she'd kept glancing at the clock. Soon, it'd be time to call Nathan. Her heart beat faster at the thought.

After printing copies of the report and stacking them on the desk, she took the elevator upstairs to her apartment. The growling of her stomach reminded her that she'd skipped lunch.

She made a vegetable salad and set the table. After she talked to Nathan, she'd grill half a chicken breast. She was too antsy to eat before.

She walked through the apartment, absentmindedly picking up objects and setting them down again. Inside her, Joshua and Jeremy responded to her nervousness by acting as if they'd taken up gymnastics. She yearned to share them with Nathan, let him hear their hearts beating, let him know these two were part of them.

At eight o'clock sharp, she sat down on the couch, took a deep breath to calm herself, and dialed his number. The phone rang three times, then his answering machine clicked in. "I have to go out of town," he said, his words nearly running over each other. "On a personal emergency. My wife's in the hospital."

Amy listened numbly to the dead line until the receiver began to make beeping sounds. She dropped it into the cradle and tried to stand up. Her legs wouldn't hold her.

His message to her had sounded so urgent, but he had left without a thought to the danger he'd told her she was in.

Oh God. *Oh God.* She clasped her stomach and shook as if she'd taken a chill.

His priority was Angela. And it always would be.

30

Amy sat beside her father in the van, staring at fir trees thrashing in the wind. The weather echoed her chaotic emotions. Nathan had told her she was in danger, then had vanished. Now, she didn't know where the threat might lie.

B.J. glanced at her with an anxious expression. "You okay?"

"Sure. Just feel a little groggy. I didn't sleep well last night." Actually, she couldn't remember having slept at all.

"Why didn't you say something? I could have made this trip by myself."

"I needed to get out of the house." She'd cried for hours but it hadn't helped. For no reason, tears filmed her eyes. She blinked them away, then her nose started to run. She groped in the oversized pocket of her raincoat for a handkerchief and brought out a small book instead.

She located a handkerchief, blew her nose and picked up the book in her lap, wondering where it'd come from. She opened the cover and peered at an inscription that read, *For Mai to keep always*—and everything came back to her.

The day she, her father, and Nathan went to the Nguyen house she'd found the paperback among the piles of ripped-up books and had put it in her pocket, intending to give it to Cam. She scanned the dog-eared child's story and remembered Mai had once told her about her father writing a story and having it made into a book.

"Whatcha got there?" B.J. asked.

"A story Chantou Pran wrote for Mai. Listen." She read about a little girl named Mai who was left all alone except for a miniature dragon with green eyes and fiery breath. He helped Mai escape from many perilous adventures with fearsome demons.

One day the little dragon was mortally wounded. As he lay dying, he asked Mai to cut open his stomach. Reluctantly, she followed his instructions and drew out the emerald green of his eyes, the ruby red of his kind heart, and the white hot heat of his fiery breath.

He asked her to care for his most precious belongings until the demons were vanquished. He made her promise that when peace once again reigned over their land, she would take the cherished objects to his father in the east.

"That's a strange tale to tell a child," B.J. said. "The dragon's left there with his innards hanging out. I wouldn't call that a happily-ever-after ending."

Amy pointed to the tattered pages. "Evidently, Mai liked the story. I'll pass it on to Cam next time I see him." Amy slipped the book into her pocket and turned to watch the passing scenery again.

* * *

When they reached Wheeler, B.J. let Amy out at Fenwick's Athletic Club and went on to the courthouse. In the club's foyer, she met Kim.

"Ah, Dr. Prescott," he said, flashing a smile. "I'm most happy to see you. Are you joining our mothers today?"

"Yes, I've been too busy to get to class lately."

"Most unfortunate. Much better, I think, if you be mother, not investigator."

She studied him, searching for evidence of a threat, and found his features as bland as before. "You may be right. Has Dr. Nguyen been in?"

He wagged his head. "I think maybe he is regretting what he did."

She fixed her gaze on him. "What did he do?"

"He said his girlfriend told his wife she was pregnant." His wife threatened to tell the hospital where he worked. That day he played handball like a madman. He hides it well, but I think he is a violent man."

Amy was momentarily at a loss for what to say. The words, 'his girlfriend told his wife she was pregnant' echoed inside her head. She pressed her hands against her chest. Was that why Cam disappeared when Chea's car was found? The thought staggered her.

"Dr. Prescott, are you all right?" Kim peered at her. "I did not wish to upset you."

"Thank you for telling me, Kim." She wandered off to the aerobics room in a daze. Had she let her friendship with Cam blind her?

She sat down on a mat and scanned the room for Hue. She nudged the woman in front of her. "Have you seen Hue Quoy?"

"She not coming," the woman said, and frowned. "Someone say she hurt."

A chill rippled up Amy's spine. "What happened?"

When the woman shrugged, Amy jumped to her feet and rushed out. A public phone hung on the wall in the foyer, but she hurried outside. She didn't want anyone overhearing her conversation.

She walked two blocks before she found a phone where she could have a little privacy. She dialed Hue's number and waited anxiously until Hue answered.

"This is Amy. What happened? Are you all right?"

"Oh, Amy. The other night, I was attacked in the grocery store parking lot."

"Were you hurt?"

"A black eye, bruises on my face, and a sprained ankle is all. But I was scared, so scared, Amy. I thought he was going to kill me, or rape me, or both. Luckily I was able to get away from him."

"Thank God, Hue. Did you see his face?"

"He had a hood over his head."

A hood! "Did you say anything to you?"

"He speaks Cambodian. He said to stay away from you and keep my mouth shut or he'd kill me."

"I shouldn't have gotten you involved. Any possibility it was Victor Samphan?"

"No, this man was shorter and slimmer and he smelled peculiar."

"Like incense?"

"Yes, yes, that's it. Did you find out who the dead woman is?"

"Her name's Chea Le. Cam claimed he was with her the night Mai was murdered."

"Are you saying he killed this Chea Le?"

"I don't know. He hasn't been seen since the day the body was found."

"He can't have killed her, Amy. That'd mean he

killed Mai too. No! I don't believe it. He couldn't have."

"I don't want to believe it either, but I have to consider the possibility. Are either you or Raymond acquainted with an Asian man with a scar on the right side of his face?"

"No, but I think I know who you mean. I saw such a man in the market the other day. He knocked down an old man who got in his way."

"Didn't anybody do anything?"

"Some men tried to grab him. He snarled at them, Amy. Just like a savage dog, then he did some karate moves and frightened them away."

"What else can you tell me about him?"

"Oh. One thing—he had a broken front tooth."

Amy's grip tightened on the receiver. *The man who'd spied on Mai from the woods. The man whose picture she had taken when he was crouched in the bushes outside Nguyen's window. The man she'd seen somewhere else in Wheeler. Somewhere, she was almost positive, he shouldn't have been.*

31

Victor Samphan sat stiffly erect, his face expressionless. Elliott Osgood, Ivan Fenwick's attorney, tilted his straight-backed chair against the wall and steepled his fingers over his abdomen.

"I hope this pays off," B.J. said in a low tone. From their vantage point in Sheriff Boyce's office, Amy and her father could see and hear what went on in the adjoining interrogation room.

"The sheriff has to get *something* out of him," Amy whispered. "We're at a dead standstill."

Sheriff Boyce stooped and flattened his palms on the small table in front of Samphan. "How long have you known Chea Le?"

"I don't."

The sheriff paced the length of the eight-foot-by-eight-foot room and swung around to face the man. "Know anything about her car going into the river less than half a mile from your house?"

"Don't answer that, Mr. Samphan," Elliott Osgood said.

Samphan smirked and sat back in his chair.

Sheriff Boyce thrust his face in close. "You killed

her, then drove her car into the byway, didn't you, Mr. Samphan?"

"Now, Fred," Osgood said.

Samphan scowled at the attorney. "I didn't know her and I didn't kill her," he said to Boyce.

"You're sure of that?" The sheriff leaned against the wall.

"You're damned right. Why the hell you accusing me? I ain't the one who's been screwin' her."

"Ah, but you know who has, don't you Victor?"

"Sure. That double-dealing doctor."

Amy frowned as a smile of satisfaction spread over the sheriff's face. "Look at him," she said. "He's still bent on pinning the whole works on Cam."

B.J. gestured for her to be silent.

"And who else?" The sheriff asked, beginning to pace again.

"How the hell should I know?"

"How'd you know about the doctor? You been spying on him?"

"Everybody in town knows." Samphan flung out his hands. "Shit! Even his wife knew it."

Boyce spun around. "Who told you that?"

"I don't know"—Samphan's voice raised an octave—"I can't remember."

"You can't *remember?*" The sheriff slammed his fist down on the table. "Was it Kim Sen?"

"No. No. He—he isn't a friend of mine, anyway. We don't talk."

"Well, now, Victor, I don't blame him much. I wouldn't befriend a liar myself." He took a turn of the room. "Matter of fact, liars make me real mad." He crouched over the man. "What about the guy with the scar? Did he know Chea Le?"

Samphan's face blanched. "No! Not him—" He gulped nervously. "I d-don't know who you're talking about."

"I think you do. You responded when I mentioned that his face was scarred."

"Y-you said—"

"What?" He narrowed his eyes. "Well, what have you got to say?"

"About what?"

The sheriff's face turned red with anger. "Don't get smart with me, you little shit. What the hell is Scarface's name?"

"I—I—" Victor glanced around, his eyes wide with terror. "I don't know w-who you're t-talking about."

Elliott Osgood languidly lifted his gaze from his steepled fingers. "You'd badgering Mr. Samphan, Fred."

"Knock it off, El. You can see this slant-eyed bastard is in this up to his goddamned balls. He knows what's been going on in my town." He scowled at Samphan. "I think I'll lock him up for a few days, then he'll spill—"

"No!" Victor Samphan leaped out of his chair and clutched Osgood's arm. "Don't let him. I can't be locked in here." He gave the attorney such a jerk he nearly fell off his chair. "I can't be. Do you hear? He'll—"

Sheriff Boyce grabbed him and threw him back on his chair. "Sit there, damn you, and don't move."

Elliott Osgood yawned, stretched, and got to his feet. "Do you have any concrete evidence against my client, Fred?"

The sheriff braced his fists on his hips. "You step out of the room for five minutes and I'll have more than enough to clear this whole damned town of gooks. You got my word on that."

Osgood wagged his head. An expression of distaste flitted over his face as his gaze came to rest on Victor. "Not that I wouldn't like to see you do just that, you understand. Unfortunately, Mr. Fenwick's paying me to protect this man." He looked up at Boyce once again. "He doesn't want the club to get any bad publicity."

Sheriff Boyce focused his steely-eyed gaze on Victor. "I'm letting you go . . . for now."

Samphan stood up, flung an insolent look at the sheriff, and swaggered toward the door.

Sheriff Boyce waited with a half smile tugging at his lips until Samphan's fingers touched the knob. "And I'll be sure to tell Scarface you told me where to find him."

32

B.J. growled and got up from the conference table. During the past three days, he and Amy had gone over every scrap of evidence they had gathered, searching for something they may have overlooked.

"This case is driving me nuts." He smacked the table. "Piles of evidence, yet we still haven't got any suspects." He stuck the folders in the file cabinet and slammed the drawer. "I have to be in court at one. I should be back in a couple of hours."

Amy levered herself out of her chair. "I think I'll clean house. I didn't get to do much organizing before Mary moved in."

"You sure having a stranger in your apartment is a good idea?"

She squared her shoulders. "She's not a stranger, and you'll like her once you get to know her."

"Aren't you overdoing this ethnic thing a trifle?"

"No," Amy said firmly, shoving the chairs into place around the conference table. "End of discussion." She marched out to the office and began clearing off her desk.

After B.J. left, Amy squatted on her heels behind the

desk, filing papers in a bottom drawer. When she heard the door open and close, she didn't even look up. "Did you forget something?" she said, thinking B.J. had returned.

"Yes," Jed said. "The rules."

Amy sighed, straightened up, and sank onto her chair. "How have you been?"

Jed picked up a brass paperweight and tossed it from one hand to the other. "Ashamed."

"Forget it. I had to put my ex-husband to bed lots of times."

"Well, it's never happened to me before and it won't happen again."

Amy looked at him skeptically. "It will if you keep drinking as heavily as you have been lately."

Jed set the paperweight on the desk. "I've stopped feeling sorry for myself."

"Keep busy, Jed. Play golf, play tennis, start a hobby. It helps fill up the slack time."

"Will you"—he squared the paperweight with the edge of a blotter without meeting her eyes—"let me see you again?"

She smiled. "Of course, we're friends, aren't we?"

He came around the desk, kissed her on the forehead, and smiled softly at her. "You're a special woman, Amy." He brushed her cheek with his fingers. "Don't ever change." When she smiled at him, he did an about-face, blew her a kiss, and sauntered out, whistling.

Amy closed the office, took the elevator upstairs to her apartment, and began to dust the furniture in the living room.

As she worked, Mary came out of her room. "Can I help?"

"No, I need the exercise. So, how's it going? Do you have enough space for your things?"

"Space? There's so much of it I feel like a bug in a barn," Mary said. "For most of my life, I've shared a room with my sisters."

"Just wait, Mary." Amy sat down on the rug and rested her back against the couch. "When the twins are born, this apartment will seem a lot smaller."

A smile lit Mary's eyes. "That'll be nice." She regarded Amy from beneath lowered lids. "We need some noise around here."

"Oh yeah." Amy laughed. "I'll remind you of that when we're each walking the floor with a crying baby in our arms."

Mary smiled, picked up her book pack, and left for the university. Amy was preparing to dust the bookcase when the phone rang. She didn't know how to feel when she heard Nathan's voice come over the line.

"Sorry I didn't call sooner," he said.

"Well, I'm still here. I guess that's a good sign." The words came out flat and cold.

Nathan remained silent for a full beat. "You're still in danger, Amy. My contact in Cambodia reports that Taun Keo, Mai Nguyen's father, was an assistant conservator at the Silver Temple in Angkor."

His voice sounded weary, and she wished she hadn't been so abrupt. "I see," she said in a much softer tone.

"When the Khmer Rouge started their killing spree in Cambodia, Keo's superior planned to use the temple's jewels to insure his and his family's safety. Taun Keo found out about the head conservator's plans, took the jewels, and disappeared with his infant daughter."

"Mai?"

"Yes. The Khmer Rouge shot the head conservator,

sent his wife to a work camp, and conscripted his two young sons into the army. My contact thinks the sons may now be in the States."

"To get revenge for what Mai's father did?"

"Yes, and to recover the jewels."

"Others have been murdered, Nathan."

"Tell me."

Amy gave him a quick report on what had happened in the investigation since she had last spoke to him and finished with, "And now we're at an impasse."

"Tell me about this Victor Samphan."

"He works nights at the athletic club and runs the Hanuman Janitorial Service during the day."

"Did you say Hanuman?"

"Yes."

"Spell it."

Amy recited the letters of the word slowly.

"That's odd," he said, half to himself. "Who are their customers?"

"Mostly Asian businesses, I think. Although I heard the athletic club uses them, so maybe some of the other Caucasian-run firms employ them too. Why?"

"The *yavana* are making the Asian merchants pay protection money, right?"

"Yes, they threaten to burn their shops if they don't."

"Amy, everywhere I went in that town the people's fear was strong."

"If somebody threatened to burn down my business, I'd be scared too."

"Every old-country Cambodian knows that a hanuman is a venomous snake. It lives in the trees, is swift as lightning, and has a nasty habit of dropping on its victims when they least expect it."

"Strange to name a cleaning service after a poisonous

nake," Amy said. "Do you think it's possible that the
wo men that had the vendetta against Mai's father are
ehind the extortion scheme too?"

"You said Mai's father was killed about six months
go. This protection racket has been going on for at
east that long. The Pham brothers would need money.
know they're not registered as aliens—I checked.
hey're probably using fake I.D.'s and aliases, but that
ets risky when it comes to owning a vehicle or getting
job."

"So they get a high-stakes gambler like Victor
amphan in debt to them and use him as a front."

"They will do whatever it takes. These men have
een trained to infiltrate, to intimidate, to torture, to kill.
liminating a human being means no more to them than
quashing a worm."

Amy shivered. "Apparently, they thought Mai's father
till had the jewels."

"And that's the reason they tortured his daughter."

"Poor Mai. Why didn't she just give them what they
vanted?"

"She probably figured they would still rape and mur-
ler her whether she told them or not."

Amy let out her breath, but it didn't relieve the heav-
ness in her chest. "Hue Quoy told me Mai's father
elped all of the Asians in one way or another. Even
ictor Samphan said Mr. Pran loaned money to those
vho needed it. Do you suppose he sold the jewels to
elp out his fellow countrymen?"

"That wouldn't be easy. Some of the finest rubies and
apphires in the world come from Cambodia. Mai's fa-
her would have to have had illicit connections in the
em community in order to sell the large stones he took.
According to the CIA, a ten-karat top quality ruby can

sell for more than two hundred thousand dollars a kara
To add to his problems, the sale of a large, perfect ge
would cause a rather conspicuous ripple in the gem ma
ket."

"So it's likely the gems are still hidden somewhere"

"From what I saw at the Nguyen house, the Pha
brothers think so."

Amy massaged a tight muscle in her neck. The new
put a different slant on the case, but still didn't tell the
who the guilty parties were. "Thank you for calling, N
than. You've been very helpful."

"Be careful, Amy, these men are dangerous."

"I will." She moistened her throat. "How is Angela"
she asked.

He drew in a breath and exhaled noisily. "Sick. Ver
sick. She has cirrhosis of the liver."

Amy sat up straighter in her chair. "But how—"

Nathan sighed. "The doctor says she's been drinkir
since she was in her early teens. She kept it und
control—she was never noticeably drunk. I didn't eve
know she had a problem until she got sick."

He let out another sigh. "I went through the apar
ment. There were bottles of vodka under the dirty laur
dry, behind the canned goods in the kitchen, in h
dresser drawers, and who knows where else."

Amy felt a stab of pain in her chest. "Perhaps that
why she didn't want to start a family."

"I will probably never know, *Mihewi.*"

"Is she"—Amy wet her lips—"at home now?"

"The doctor says she must stop drinking or she wi
die. She'll remain at a treatment center until they fe
she can function without alcohol." He paused for a me
ment. When he spoke again, he sounded bone-wear
"The doctor could not tell me how long that will take

"I'm sorry, Nathan."

"Don't waste your sympathy on me," he said in a harsh voice. "I don't deserve it."

They hung up shortly after that.

Although her conversation with Nathan had drained her, Amy doggedly attacked the bookcase, trying to get her mind off the concern she felt for him. She dusted and rearranged as she proceeded from one shelf to the next, upsetting a photo album in the process. As she started to transfer the album to a closed cupboard, a number of pictures spilled out onto the floor.

Swearing under her breath, Amy got down on her hands and knees. The first picture she picked up was one she'd taken at Mai and Cam's wedding.

She studied the smiling couple. They stood in Mai's garden, their hands linked, their eyes shining. Behind them, silhouetted against the sky, was the topiary castle and dragon Mai's father had created for his beloved daughter.

The dragon! Mai's father might have suggested the ceremony take place in the topiary garden so Mai would always have her wedding pictures to remind her ...

Amy ran to the closet, took Mai's storybook from her coat pocket, and sat down to read part of the tale again: *"You must cut open my stomach," the dragon said in a faint voice. "No, no," Mai cried, but her friend persisted until she did as he asked. "Draw out my emerald green eyes," he said. "My ruby red heart and the white, hot heat of my breath.*

Amy stopped and stared at the photo again. Could Mai's father have had a twofold purpose in writing the story?

She flipped back to the first page and read again—
For Mai to keep always. She leafed through the book
again until another sentence caught her eye. *When peace
is restored to our land return these precious belonging.
to my father in the East.*

He'd said something similar in the sealed letter Je.
had taken from Chantou's safety deposit box. Amy hurried to the office, opened the case file, and scanned thei.
copy of the letter. She reread the part that seemed incon
sistent with the general purpose of his message.

*When Kampuchea is free of the nightmare and Bud
dha can once again look upon beauty. Then I beseech
you to remember your favorite childhood game and re
store the Enlightened One's sight.*

She heard the foyer door bang shut and B.J. walke.
into the office. "Still at it?" he said. "I thought you wer.
going to clean house."

She regarded him with a triumphant smile. "We hav.
to go to Wheeler. I know what those men are lookin;
for, Dad." Her smile broadened. "And I know where t.
find it."

33

"Look." Sheriff Boyce leaned across his desk and pointed his finger at B.J. and Amy. "I hauled in Victor Samphan because you two got a wild hair and what did it get me? Now you come in here talking about fairy stories."

Amy reined in her growing impatience. "Central Intelligence suspects that—" She halted, thinking she heard a noise in the corridor leading to the jail. She didn't want her conversation to be overheard. She paused and glanced down the hallway. When the sound wasn't repeated, she continued. "The CIA thinks the Pham brothers have come to the United States to find the temple jewels, the loss of which got their father killed."

"Temple jewels!" Sheriff Boyce flung up his hands. "Good God, what next?" He thrust out his beefy jaw. "So where do you suggest I find these jewel hunters?"

Amy ignored his heavy sarcasm. "They're probably using assumed names, so I don't—. Yes, I do, actually. Remember the apartment house where Dr. Nguyen and Chea Le were supposed to have gone? The manager's name is Pham! He's probably a relative. That would explain why he helped frame Cam."

Boyce folded his arms across his chest. "I don't happen to think he was framed, Missy."

"Sheriff, Amy thinks she knows where the jewels are hidden," B.J. said in a conciliatory tone. "We'd like you to come along."

Amy scooted forward on her chair. "Then you can see for yourself how all the pieces fit together."

"No way am I going to be a part of this screw-loose scheme. I'd be the laughingstock of the town."

Amy stood up. "Okay, if that's the way you feel. I'm still going over to the Nguyens' to—" She paused abruptly upon hearing the clank of a bucket in the hallway. Suddenly, from out of her subconscious rose a face she'd seen the first time she'd visited Cam. "He's here!"

Amy rushed to the office door and looked down the corridor. At the far end, a man in gray striped coveralls peered back at her nervously, jerked open a door, and darted through it. She swung back around to the two men. "That man must be taken into custody."

"What the hell are you talking about?" Boyce exclaimed.

"The man with the scarred face you were trying to get Victor Samphan to name. He's your janitor."

"That scrawny little gook? You gotta be kidding."

"Look, dammit." Amy rushed to the window and pointed to a dilapidated gray van as it made a tire-squealing turn onto Main Street and disappeared in the fog. "He works for the Hanuman Janitorial Service."

"I know that. So what?"

She repeated Nathan's assertion about the extortion scheme.

Sheriff Boyce laughed. "Jesus Christ, girl, nobody's puttin' the squeeze play on anybody. If they were, I'd know about it."

Her patience snapped. "If you got off your rear end and talked to some of the Asians you'd—"

"Now just a goddamned minute"—Sheriff Boyce rose out of his chair so fast it rolled backwards and crashed into the wall—"No smart-mouthed woman is going to tell me how to run my department."

"Now, Sheriff." B.J. stood up and moved between them. "My daughter is just a little upset. This case has all of us on edge."

"Don't try to sweet-talk me, Prescott. I've had it with the both of you. Now get the hell out of here and let me get some work done."

"You shouldn't let your temper get the best of you, Amy," B.J. said as soon as they were outside.

"Look who's talking." Amy hauled herself into the passenger seat of his van and slammed the door. "I just can't believe it. The man we're looking for has been right under our noses all this time. Why didn't I realize it sooner?"

"Don't be so hard on yourself. Janitors are invisible." B.J. started the engine. "We'd better get a move on. It'll be dark soon."

When B.J. brought the van to a stop in the Nguyens' driveway, he pulled his pistol from his shoulder holster. "Let me take a look around first. If that man overheard us talking in the sheriff's office, they know we're here."

Amy took out her .38. In that case, we'll go together." She slung the strap of her tote bag around her neck and clambered out of the van. Heavy leaden clouds hung low in the sky. Tattered blankets of fog draped the shrubbery and condensation dripped from the eaves, pinging on an overturned wheelbarrow below.

B.J. stiffened his arms and wheeled in a slow forty-five-degree turn. "We could do without this damned fog."

Each on the alert, they edged along the garage wall until they reached the rear corner. Amy peered toward the grove of trees where the men had spied on Mai. "Surely they wouldn't have the guts to try something in broad daylight."

"I'd sure feel a hell of a lot better if Boyce had come along for backup."

"Some backup. He'd probably shoot us all in the foot." She crouched down. "You all set?"

"Keep low when we get into the open, Amy. I'll cover you."

She flung an exasperated look over her shoulder. "No heroics, Dad. Let's go." Zigzagging in a crouched position, she headed for Mai's topiary garden.

Making it to the hedge, she pressed her body into its shelter while she took deep breaths that smelled of thyme crushed underfoot. Webs of gray mist clung to topiary peacocks, rabbits, and squirrels; they appeared to be floating in the air.

B.J. crouched down beside her, puffing noisily. "Gotta get rid of some of this weight. It slows me down."

She grinned. "Hold that thought."

She pushed open the gate and hunkered down inside. The drifting mist made it difficult for her to get her bearings. Her gaze followed the hemlock balls, urns, and cubes that adorned the top of the hedge at regular intervals.

"Look," she said, pointing to the far end of the plot. "There's the castle and the dragon."

Keeping close to the hedge, she assumed a half-bent

stance and shuffled through tall, wet grass. The sodden
legs of her slacks flapped against her boots.

Although her back ached and she longed to straighten
up, she knew it would be foolish to risk it. She arrived
at her destination, holstered her gun, and took the tote
bag strap from around her neck.

B.J. crouched down beside her. "I have a bad feeling
about this. Let's make short work of it."

Amy reached up and felt along the base of the
dragon. "No such luck, Dad. These yew limbs are
wound in and around a chicken-wire frame." She
handed B.J. a pair of wire cutters and she took up the
pruning shears. "I'm afraid we'll have to do most of
the cutting by feel."

B.J. held apart the dark green foliage while she
wielded the shears. "I hope you're right about this.
Boyce would love it if we came up with nothing."

"Mai's last words were, 'my garden.' She must have
been attempting to tell Cam something important."

Amy tried to work quickly, but the yew needles
prickled and the branches were tough and knotted with
age. When she'd cleared a small opening, she stood
back while B.J. cut into the mass of wires.

She glanced up at the sky. "It's getting darker by the
minute."

"We can't stop now. They could be here any minute."
B.J. stepped aside. "Your turn."

"I'll bet our friendly janitor's read every report I've
sent to the sheriff."

"If that's the case, they're well aware of how close
we're getting."

"Maybe that'll make them a little cautious." She
stuck her forefinger into the tiny gap in the branches

they'd made. "I think . . ." She changed the position of her hand. "Yes! There's something in there."

"Let me see." He pushed his finger into the hole. "You're right, there is." He wielded the nippers with increased vigor.

Inch by hard-won inch, they widened the gap. "I can't see what I'm doing, Amy. Did you bring a flashlight?"

"No, I didn't think we'd need one." She slid her hand inside to estimate the dimensions of the plastic-covered bundle. "If I cut a few of the branches at the sides, maybe you can pry the frame apart."

Fumbling in the half-dark, she snipped here, slashed there. "Try it now." The silence hung heavily in the air between them.

B.J. grunted as he pried. "Ouch, stabbed my hand on a wire." The hedge rustled as he grappled the underbelly of the dragon. "Now. Get the thing out of there."

"I have a grip on it, Dad." Wire scraped her skin. Sharp limbs stabbed her. "But I don't think I can get—"

"Quick, Amy. I can't hold this much longer."

She gave the parcel a jerk. It snagged on a branch. When she yanked it again, the parcel came free so abruptly, she fell back on her rear end. "We've got them, Dad! We've got the temple jewels."

"Maybe. Maybe not. Could be a red herring. Let's get out of here and see what's in that thing."

Amy tossed their tools and the parcel in the tote bag and drew her gun. "I'm ready when you are."

B.J. led the way, stopping every few minutes to peer into the gloom. They passed through the garden gate and started at a dead run for the protection of the garage.

Suddenly, the crack of a rifle sounded and a bullet

ricocheted off a garden tractor nearby. "Get down!" Amy yelled. Bullets rained all around her.

"We're in for it now," B.J. muttered.

Amy instinctively felt for the medicine bag she'd promised Nathan she would always wear. *Nothing! No magic herbs. No spirits helper. Nothing to protect the twins.* She froze.

"Move, Amy!"

B.J.'s voice spurred her into action. She crawled through the grass, her pulse thundering in her ears, hoping rows of heeled-in rhododendrons would screen them from the rifleman's sight.

A bullet thunked into a stepping stone in front of her. She slunk lower, the fog and fading daylight making the sniper's aim random.

B.J. dodged behind an upright oil barrel an instant before a bullet clanged its metal side.

A bullet snipped a twig off a bush beside Amy's head. She dug her elbows into the dank sawdust mulch and inched forward. Now, ten feet of flat ground lay between her and the garage.

B.J. aimed a volley of shots at the trees. "Run, Amy. Run!"

34

B.J. hunched over the wheel as the van leaned into another winding curve. "See anybody, Amy? I don't dare take my eyes off the road in this damned fog."

Amy turned and glanced behind them for the fifteenth time in the last thirty-five minutes. Only three cars had passed them since they left Wheeler, and none of them had proven to be a threat.

"I see a light." She watched with growing apprehension as the light came closer. When a helmeted motorcyclist roared by without slackening his speed, she took a relieved breath.

When they entered the city limits of Ursa Bay a short time later, Amy checked behind them once again. "Maybe they didn't follow us after all."

B.J. shook his head. "Hard to believe. They've killed four people to get their hands on the parcel we found."

"If someone reported the gunfire," the police could have apprehended them before they got away."

"I don't think we can count on that." They reached a wide street lined with houses and illuminated with tall mercury vapor lights. B.J. turned his head and smiled at Amy. "Looks like we made it, kitten."

She smiled back. "I was afraid we wouldn't for a while there."

"Me too."

They fell silent as B.J. drove through the main section of town and turned onto Endicott Street.

Amy winced as one of the twins gave her a lusty kick. She patted her abdomen. *Relax, boys. I promise I won't take you on any more dangerous journeys.*

B.J. guided the van through the alley between two buildings and wheeled into their parking lot. He smacked the steering wheel. "The damned floodlight has gone out again," he said.

Amy picked up her tote bag. "Leave the headlights on until I get the dead bolt undone."

"Hang on." B.J. retrieved a five-cell torch from under the seat. "I'd better come with you. The car lights hardly make a dent in this fog." He got out on his side and closed the door.

Amy opened hers and got out to meet him, but there was no sign of her father as she closed the van door. "Dad? . . ." she called out hesitantly. She moved to the rear of the van. "Dad, where are—"

Suddenly, out of the fog, a dark mass sprang at her. She ducked and recoiled. The hooded man's blow smacked the side of the van.

Flinging the tote bag under the van, Amy drew her gun. She fired and missed. The man spun around, lashing out at her with his foot. The impact knocked her gun out of her hand and sent her reeling. She fell back against the side of the van.

The man sprang at her again. "Where are they?" he growled, pinning her against the van.

"What have you done to my father?" Amy demanded.

The side of the man's hand smashed into her head. "Answer me."

She staggered and caught hold of the door handle. "If you hurt him, you'll pay with your life."

He shoved his forearm against her throat. "Tell me where they are or I'll slit you open."

She rammed her knee into the man's groin and, as he started to crumple, bashed his nose with her head. He collapsed in a moaning heap.

Amy then rushed for the back door. Before she reached it, another hooded man grabbed her arm and spun her around to face him.

"Give me the jewels."

Not hesitating for a moment, she drove the point of her key into the back of his hand. When he cried out and loosened his grip, she jerked free and dashed for the alley.

Recovering, the man pursued and overcame her, flinging her up against the building. Amy saw the glint of a knife. "Give them to me," the man snarled.

"No!" Amy yelled and jammed her heel down on his toes.

He let out a bellow of rage and grabbed her by the throat. "Want me to slice you open and cut out your baby?"

Immediately, she stopped struggling. *What was she doing?* Too much was at stake. "In a bag under the van," she said.

Her assailant barked a command in the direction of the van. Amy heard a groan as the other man dragged himself to all fours and crawled toward the car.

But as he neared it, another man leaped out of the darkness. Amy watched as the man by the car was whacked in the head with a gun. She immediately recognized the gunman's walk as he turned and approached them.

"Let go of her, or I'll blow a hole clear through you."

Relief surged through her. "Easy, Cam. He's got a knife."

"Stupid white bitch!" Her assailant snarled. Lunging forward, he delivered a blow to her ribs, wheeled, and ran.

Amy gasped for breath and slid down the wall until she came to rest on the asphalt.

She heard Cam's gun fire, then an agonized cry as the fleeing man pitched forward, then struggled to rise. "My leg, my leg!" he screamed.

Cam ran to him, yanked off the man's hood, and jammed his gun barrel against the man's belly. "Make a move, you dirty sonofabitch. I'm just itching to put a bullet in your gut and watch you suffer even more."

"Cam?" Amy called weakly. "They have my father . . ."

Cam peered into the fog. "I'll be there as soon as I get these two tied up, Amy."

Just then, B.J. wandered out from around the van, rubbing his head. "Amy?" he called.

"Dad!" she said thankfully.

"You all right?" he asked.

A siren wailed in the distance. "Cam"—she drew in a shallow breath and pain lanced through her chest—"give . . . your gun . . . to my father . . . before the police get here."

Cam glared at the men on the pavement and handed his pistol to B.J., who wiped the gun clean, and stuck the gun in his jacket pocket. "I'll take care of these men; please stay with my daughter until the police arrive."

Cam dropped down beside her. "Did he hurt you?"

She struggled for breath. "He . . . hit . . . me."

"Where?"

"Left side."

Cam turned her toward the light. "Jesus!" He shucked his jacket and took off his shirt, popping buttons in his haste. "Dr. Prescott, she's got a knife in her ribs."

"What?" B.J. exclaimed, leaping up from where he sat wrapping duct tape around the men's hands and feet. He ran over to her. "Do something, Cam. You're the trauma expert."

Cam unzipped her coat, ripped open her blouse, and pressed his folded shirt to the wound. "I need tape and bandages."

Amy clutched Cam's arm. "I'm pregnant with twins." Pain exploded inside her and ballooned outward.

"How far along?"

"Eighteen weeks." She bit down on her lip until she tasted blood. Every word burned like fire, but she had to make sure. "Don't . . . let the doctors . . . do anything"—she paused to gather her strength—"that'll harm the babies."

B.J. skidded to a halt beside her. "Hang in there, Amy. I called 911." He snapped open his medical bag, spread open a towel, and laid out the things Cam would need. He held his torch while Cam worked over Amy.

Cam's gaze met hers. "The knife has to stay where it is until we get you to the hospital."

Cold sweat broke out on her forehead and she fought down a wave of weakness. "I . . . understand."

B.J. squatted down and pressed his hand against her cheek. "Hang in there, kitten. Hang in there."

"I'll make it, Dad. I have to."

Cam tore open a packet of four-by-four gauze

sponges and crammed them around the knife handle to stem the flow of blood. Every few minutes, he tossed sodden gauze aside, added a clean pack, and applied pressure.

She groaned as a fiery torment wracked her chest.

"Sorry, Amy. This has to be done." He taped the bandages and knife securely in place.

B.J. shifted from one foot to the other. "When is that damned ambulance going to get here?"

Amy heard a door slam, the sound of running footsteps, and then saw Mary Little Bear's anxious face above her. "Is she all right?"

"She's been stabbed," Cam said. "Did you see what happened?"

"Yes, I live with Amy. I was in my room"—she pointed up at her window—"I saw them attack her and called the police." She turned to stare at the two bound men. "Who are they?"

"Kim and Tai Sen," Cam said without looking up.

"Their real name is Pham," B.J. said. "Their father was conservator of a temple in Cambodia. Mai's father was his assistant. The conservator planned to give the temple jewels to the Khmer Rouge in exchange for his family's safety. Chantou Pran found out, took the jewels, and he and Mai left the country."

"Chantou Pran!" Tai Pham sneered derisively, his mouth twisted into an evil leer "Tuan Keo. Thief! Murderer!" Tai spat out a stream of Khmer invective. "He stole our father, our mother." He touched his scar. "Our lives. The temple jewels belong to *us.*"

The sirens drew closer. Revolving blue and red lights created kaleidoscopic patterns in the fog.

"Let me go," Kim pleaded. "I have done nothing."

Cam shook his fist at him. "Nothing! Sadistic

sonofabitch. You raped and murdered my wife. You killed Chea Le. You came close to killing Amy!"

"Lying *yuon* scum. Tai did it, not me."

"Like hell! Chea told me she was pregnant. That her lover lived in Wheeler." Cam rolled his coat and propped up Amy to ease her breathing. "After they found Chea, I followed you. I heard you and Tai talking."

A moment after two police cars and an emergency vehicle roared up the alley, two medics converged on Amy. B.J. squeezed his daughter's hand. "You're going to be fine, honey. Just fine." His worried expression contrasted with his words.

"Dad," she said, her voice barely a whisper. "Nathan mustn't find out about—"

Then Darkness closed in on her.

35

Amy struggled out of oblivion and opened her eyes. Nathan sat beside her bed, his face as rigid as if he'd been carved in stone. His head thrown back, his eyes closed, his lips moving silently, he tapped a steady rhythm on his thigh.

She lay still. She could not seem to think straight; her thoughts flooded together incoherently. Then a dark shaft of pain bore down on her. Sweat beaded her face and trickled from her scalp onto the damp pillow. An agonized moan started in the pit of her stomach and worked its way up to her lips.

Nathan started, slowly lifted his lids, and gazed at her.

"I . . . hurt," she murmured, touching her chest.

"I know."

She took a shallow breath and fire seared her lungs. A tear ran down her cheek.

Nathan lifted his hand as if to reach out, then he stiffened and drew back. "They're unable to give you any more for the pain," he said in a harsh, tight voice. "Because of the pregnancy."

He knew. "Nathan . . ." she said. "Am I—are they—

all right?" She lay her hand on his arm. He stared at her with a bleak expression and nodded. "The doctor says you will make a full recovery. The babies are unharmed." She let her hand fall back on the bed. "Thank God," she said. "Did my father call you?"

He shook his head. "I was asleep, I woke up . . . and I knew. I called your home and a young woman told me you were in the hospital. I caught the first plane to Seattle."

"Nathan . . . I forgot to put your medicine pouch around my neck this morning." She smiled weakly. "This"—she gestured to the hospital bed—"is all my fault."

He patted her arm, heaved a sigh, and got to his feet. "Other people want to see you." He gave her a sheepish glance. "I have not let anyone in except the nurse and the doctor. Not even your father. Neither he nor your"—he grimaced—"your redheaded male friend is very happy with me."

She started to laugh, then winced as pain seared her chest.

He took her hand. "Easy now. You okay?"

She clenched her teeth until the spasm passed, leaving her body wet with perspiration. "Thank you," she said in a wan voice.

He dampened a washcloth and ran it over her face. "You should have told me you were pregnant."

"I . . . I thought you—"

"I understand." The skin drew tight over his cheeks and whitened around his mouth. "I'm glad you found someone else you could be close to. Are you happy, Amy?"

Amy's breath caught in her throat. "He . . . he doesn't know." *And now he never would.*

Nathan looked at her with a puzzled expression. "There is no love between you?"

She fought to clear the fogginess from her brain. Were they really having this conversation or was it some bad dream?

She let her feelings from him shine in her eyes. "How could there be love between us?"

He leaned down and pressed his cheek against hers. "Try to rest." He straightened. "I'll send in your father."

A cold lump gathered in her stomach. "Will you be back?"

"Yes. In a little while."

Immediately after he strode out, B.J. hurried to her bedside. "How do you feel, kitten?"

"Kind of shaky." She clutched his hand and let out her breath. "My chest hurts like fury."

B.J. nodded. "I'm not surprised. You've got rather a bad chest wound."

"Did the police arrest Cam?"

B.J. smiled. "Jed and I have had several meetings with Captain Moretti, Prosecuting Attorney Ingalls, and Sheriff Boyce.

"Tai Pham's bite impression is the same as the one the forensic dentist took off the piece of candy you found by the stakeout site. His fingerprints correspond with those in Nguyen house and on the back of Chea Le's car. And I'll bet both of the brothers' DNA matches the semen I found in Mai's vagina." He regarded her closely. "Am I tiring you?"

"Go on. I'll rest better once I know."

B.J. nodded. "Kim's fingerprints match those in the Nguyen house, also those on the interior and exterior of Chea's car." He smiled at her. "He's flat-footed and has a triangular scar on his right heel like the impressions you took at Cam's house. And I'm as sure as I'm standing here that his DNA will be identical with the tissue under Mai's nails and will prove he was the father of Chea's unborn baby."

"What about the knife?" Amy asked.

"The one Kim stabbed you with is the same one he used to kill Mai."

She lay back against her pillow. "And the jewels? Were they in the package we found in Mai's garden?"

"I'll say." B.J.'s eyes snapped with excitement. "Honey, I've never seen gems the size of those. The rubies were damned near as big as cherries."

He stopped and smoothed back her damp hair. "Now you've got to rest awhile. Jed wants to say a quick hello, then we'll leave you alone."

After B.J. retreated, Jed entered with a belligerent set to his jaw. "Who the hell does that big black-haired dude think he is? He acts as if he owns you."

"He's a very dear old friend," Amy said.

"Well, he can get his ass back to where he belongs. I can look after you and the twins. And—" He stopped in midsentence as Amy groaned and clamped her mouth close to keep from crying out.

"Oh, I'm sorry, Amy, I'm sorry." He sank down onto a chair. "I don't know what's wrong with me." He ran his hand over his face. "I got so damned steamed. I forgot how much pain you're in." He patted her arm. "I'll get out of here so you can go back to sleep."

When Amy woke up several hours later, she found a pink bed jacket lying at the foot of her bed. An attached note said, *Thought you might want this. Love you, Dad.*

Amy asked the nurse to brush her hair, help her into the bed jacket, and raise the head of the bed. After she left, Amy rearranged the jacket in an effort to conceal her protruding abdomen. Out of sight, out of mind, she hoped. It would be best for both of them if Nathan continued to believe she was pregnant with someone else's children.

When Nathan arrived, he stood at the foot of her bed and gazed at her intensely.

"Do you have any idea how pretty you are?"

"Pretty?" Amy pushed at a lock of limp hair. "You've got to be kidding."

He came around to the side of the bed. "Your father and I have had a long talk."

She widened her eyes in alarm. "What about?"

"You. What you were like growing up."

"Why?"

"I wanted to know. He brought albums of pictures. Told me about how your mother walked out when you were only eleven. Told me about you graduating from college with honors and about the trials of your marriage."

She let out a relieved sigh. "Pretty boring, huh?"

"Never." He reached out a tentative hand and fingered the edge of her bed jacket. "I learned something from your father."

Amy was immediately alert. *Now* what had he done? "You'll have to excuse Dad. He gets pretty wound up when it comes to me."

"He loves you, Amy. He'd make any sacrifice for you—if it came to that."

"Wouldn't most parents?"

"Only the good ones." He drew a deep breath, then another. "After listening to him talk, I realized how lucky it was that we didn't marry. You're so strong, Amy, so independent. I would have been too possessive of you."

She opened her mouth to argue and remembered his feverish plea the night they'd made love. *Only me, Amy. Only me.*

"Maybe you're right." She patted her abdomen. "And now I'm going to have lots of things vying for my attention."

He smiled sadly. "Yes. And you have so much to give." He unbuttoned his shirt, took her hand, and pressed her open palm to his chest—skin to skin. "You will always be *inmi tumnami.*" His dark eyes bored into hers. "In my heart." He leaned down and brushed her lips with his. "I will never forget you, *Mihewi.*"